PHANTOM VOICES IN TIBET

PHANTOM VOICES IN TIBET

Dick + Judy —
I hope you enjoy this.

June Calender

June Calender

CREATIVE ARTS BOOK COMPANY

Berkeley ● California

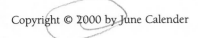
Phantom Voices in Tibet is published by Donald S. Ellis
and distributed by Creative Arts Book Company.

For information contact:
Creative Arts Book Company
833 Bancroft Way
Berkeley, California 94710
(800) 848-7789

ISBN 088739-240-7
Library of Congress Catalog Number 98-83085

Printed in the United States of America

ACKNOWLEDGEMENTS

Good fortune put me in the hands of the tour guide I call BK and his partner YD so that I was able to experience Tibet in the company of caring and kind people. My flesh and blood companions on both trips were also extraordinary people who were a pleasure to travel with in that country.

Further good fortune brought me Sienna Craig as editor for my manuscript. She was able to correct the erratic spellings of Tibetan names and words thanks to her knowledge of Tibet and the Tibetan language. Her feeling for what I wanted to say in this book was an inspiration. I've had important help from Rachel Todoroff who extracted the illustrations for this book from my amateur photographs. Leslie Roesch was a great help with the manuscript and Lynn Parpard did much appreciated photographic work.

... one would like to add some small arch
to the bridge of understanding between East and West ...

Freya Stark,
A Winter in Arabia

Five Ghosts Meet Nearly Three Miles Above Sea Level

On a barren Himalayan pass swept by relentless, bone-chilling winds, travelers have built a cairn. Into this monument are set *latzas*, slender poles lifting prayer flags, blue, green, yellow, red and white. The colors symbolize the elements water, earth, air, fire, and space in the Tibetan religion. Wind constantly snaps and twists them, carrying praise of Buddha aloft.

The British colonel, L. Austine Waddell, arrives, weary from the climb but stiff and proudly erect. He raises binoculars to his eyes and surveys the torturous path that leads down to a river valley. He ignores a small woman in peasant dress, who approaches him. She carries a bundle of belongings, using a staff to support her as she climbs, with her is a boyish *lama* also carrying a bundle. They appear to be Tibetan pilgrims. "*La gyalo!*" they shout to the wind as they pick up stones and place them on the pile. The lama moves away and sits on the ground, resting, praying.

The colonel's lip curls in disdain at the superstitiousness of "these people." He speaks to himself with considerable pride, "We were the first, well, except for the *pundits*—but they worked for us."

"As your King James had his scholars translate, 'pride goeth before a fall.'" The "pilgrim" woman's English has a marked French accent.

Col. Waddell studies her, seeing European features beneath the dirt on her tanned face. "I say, you must be that French woman." She is "that French woman," Alexandra David-Neel, but she doesn't choose to answer the question, not when asked in that tone of voice by a soldier of the King of England.

"You weren't first to invade Tibet, just the worst—puny bullies from that garbage heap of an island at the back door of Europe. I despise your exclusionary rules." She spits at his feet, but the colonel's attention has been caught by a Tibetan lady approaching on a mule, its harness decorated with the gold insignia of high rank.

The lady speaks to Alexandra, gently, with tears in her voice. "The British were not the worst, no, not at all. The Chinese have destroyed everything...everything that was lovely and good and fine."

"That was thirty-five years after I was here...but I read about it in the newspapers, Madame, and I wept for the land I love more than any place else on the earth," Alexandra replies.

The lady takes Alexandra's hand. "I wish I had known you."

A tall American approaches on the road Waddell took. He has a ruddy, untrimmed beard, blue eyes as clear as the waters of *Yomdok Tso*, the large lake that can be seen looking south from this high pass. He wears a gold brocaded *chubba*, an expensive Leica camera hangs by a strap around his neck. The lady's face loses its sadness and lights up when she sees him. She claps her hands together, her frown changes to a smile, making her look like a younger woman who has not yet witnessed the terrible things she and Alexandra were thinking of as they held hands. "Theos! Welcome back."

"Mary-la," he exclaims, "It's wonderful to see you again."

The lady's name is Rinchen Dolma Taring but she is called Mary-la by her English-speaking friends. She turns to Alexandra and says, "This is my friend, the White Lama. The American who learned to speak our language and read our religious books and who worships Buddha—as you do, Alexandra. My husband and I talked and laughed with him over pots and pots of tea. Alexandra David-Neel, this is Theos Bernard."

Alexandra gives Theos an appraisal as only a French woman of a certain age can give a younger man. Theos takes the hand Alexandra offers him and shakes it instead of kissing it as she had hoped.

"Madame Neel, what a shame—"

"*David*-Neel, please."

"Sorry. It's a shame we had to wait for a writer's mind in which to meet. I read your books that were available in English and studied with your lama at Lachen in Sikkim."

"Oh, so you were a serious student?"

"At least as serious as you yourself."

"And did the Lachen *Gompchen* teach you all the secrets he taught me?"

"Not as many as you say you learned."

Alexandra's eyes flash. Even in the afterlife she is not taken as seriously as she believes she should be. "Well, I believe that by the end of the century everybody interested in Tibet knows my name and reads my books—at least if they go to a little trouble to find them. I don't believe you are known at all." She turns to Rinchen Dolma. "Madame, do you mean to tell me you liked this young man?"

"Oh yes, we had wonderful fun together. We were young, we talked about a wonderful future for Tibet. My sister arranged that he would stay at Tsarong House while he was in Lhasa."

"Just when was this?" Alexandra asks.

"June through October 1937," Theos answers.

The colonel, who has been watching mountain eagles through his binoculars, turns his attention to Theos. "I say, young man, how DID you get permission to spend a summer in Central Tibet?"

"I asked nicely. In their language. I had friends, like Mary-la's sister, in places of influence and...I was welcomed warmly everywhere and shown secret places none of you Englishmen ever saw. I could prove it because

I photographed everything but..." his voice drops to a regretful sigh, "most of my photographs are lost now." He pauses because Waddell has narrowed his eyes and pursed his lips as if listening to a bragging schoolboy. Their gazes lock. They are the same height, their jaws are equally firm. Theos decides to add, "And perhaps, just perhaps, the lamas believed I am a reincarnation of Guru Rinpoche."

"Who?" Waddell snaps.

"Guru Rinpoche is the saint who brought Buddhism to Tibet," Alexandra says sharply, her tone implying that anyone interested in Tibet should know this. "Perhaps you've heard him called Padmashambava, his Sanskrit name."

"Saint? I say, that's a bit thick."

"However," Alexandra mutters looking at Theos, "Clothes do not make the man. Dressing like a *rinpoche* does not mean—"

"A reincarnation—*Gott in himmel!*" exclaims a resonant baritone belonging to the Austrian who has struggled up the pass to join this group of phantoms. He is driving a yak loaded with bundles. Rinchen Dolma claps her hands again in delight.

Theos and Waddell stop bickering to take the measure of the ragged mountaineer.

"You're here too, Heinrich! What a wonderful gathering. Oh, but I have no servants with me to make tea for us all. I do apologize. We should have tea." Rinchen Dolma feels responsible for providing proper Tibetan hospitality, but here she is, alone, fleeing Tibet with almost nothing to eat and only a mule driver helping her escape to India. "You haven't met the others. Let me introduce you. Heinrich Harrer, this is Theos Bernard who stayed at Tsarong House in 1937."

"I stayed there a few years later."

"A fine, forward-thinking man, Tsarong," Theos says.

"Yes, I enjoyed his company," Heinrich agrees.

"The kindest of men," the Rinchen Dolma says of her sister's husband.

4

"Theos was coming to see us again in '48 but..." Rinchen Dolma pauses, tears come to her eyes.

"I was killed. Very prematurely." He shrugs. "There's nothing more to say. Of course I wish it weren't so."

"We were looking forward to seeing you and I would certainly have introduced you two," Rinchen Dolma says.

Theos and Heinrich shake hands. "I want to introduce you to Alfschnaiter—" He looks around only to see that his companion has gone after the straying yak. "Well, later, perhaps."

Col. Waddell finds the travel-worn Austrian a considerable curiosity. "What strings did *you* pull?"

"None whatsoever. I trusted the Tibetans to give asylum to a refugee unjustly thrown into a British prisoner-of-war camp in India. I was no one's enemy."

"You Krauts were bombing London day and night, bent on the utter destruction of England."

"I was a teacher and mountaineer."

"It's over, gentlemen. It's history—only one part of the horrible events of this century," Alexandra's voice is weak with weariness. The weight of all that she saw in her hundred years on Earth bends her into a sad gnome of a woman.

In exasperation at being in the company of such unsympathetic travelers, Waddell spits out, "Why the bloody Hell have we been brought here, willy-nilly anyway? Why are we being introduced to one another in this God forsaken no man's land of a writer's imagination?"

Rinchen Dolma, always gentle, speaks quietly, "We're here to help the writer explain what Tibet was like early in the twentieth century, before the Chinese destroyed our way of life."

"She could have had worse guides. God knows, there's a lot to understand," Theos says. "And besides, she's one of the few who remember me now. It's high time someone searched the mountain ravine where my body was thrown so hastily and unceremoniously and put some flesh on my broken bones. I'm ready for a reincarnation. It's not a moment too soon."

"Never imagine it'll be all about you, old man," says Waddell, "These women writers really only write about themselves. You've read Madam Neel's work—"

"*David*-Neel, please. Of course, we write about ourselves. And you did too, Col. Waddell. Your personality comes through in every adjective and adverb."

Waddell snorts. "Why doesn't she get on with it?" Why? Because you've all invaded my imagination. Shush-shush, I'll show you Tibet today and you'll tell me what you saw. I hope to create a whole picture, past and present, something tourists usually don't see.

Before my two trips to Tibet, in October 1995 and May/June 1996, which are interwoven here like strangely joined twins, most of my curiosity about Tibet was inspired by Barbara and Michael Foster's biography of Alexandra David-Neel, *Forbidden Journey*, and by Theos Bernard's *Penthouse of the Gods*. I found a Dover reprint of L. Austine Waddell's *Lhasa and Its Mysteries: With a Record of the British Tibetan Expedition of 1903-04* about the time I decided on the trip. At the beginning of my journey, in Kathmandu's Pilgrim's Book House, I found Heinrich Harrer's two books, *Seven Years In Tibet* and *Return to Tibet*, and Rinchen Dolma Taring's *Daughter of Tibet*. My life was full of much else so my homework for my first trip was haphazard. But, I found, it was considerably more extensive than that of my companions.

I have a book which shows ancient sites (the Roman Forum, the Parthenon, etc.) as today's visitor sees them and has a plastic overlay page that fills in the missing buildings of antiquity. Likewise, my ghost guides to Tibet have given me an album of vivid verbal pictures of the past, plus many photographs, which become my overlays as I write about visiting this Chinese-occupied country with it's nearly destroyed monasteries and mutilated culture.

Alexandra David-Neel is my favorite traveler, though by no means the most helpful guide. I am inspired by her courage. At my age, fifty-five, disguised as a pilgrim, she set out on a nine-month, two thousand mile journey on foot to slip undetected into Lhasa. She had studied Buddhism in Sikkim and Shigatse, and was knowledgable enough to have earned the title *jetsuma* (learned lady). She had met the Thirteenth Dalai Lama when he was briefly in exile in Sikkim. He had suggested she visit Lhasa but Chinese and British authorities who were "protecting" Tibet from foreigners denied her travel permits.

Dressed as a Tibetan pilgrim, this intrepid Frenchwoman traveled entirely on foot accompanied by a young *lama*, Yongden. To escape detection, they often walked all night and slept in a hidden spot during the day and thus eluded the Tibetan officials who regularly turned back foreign travelers on the road to Lhasa. They begged for food, although under her robes Alexandra wore a necklace of gold coins given her by the Raja of Sikkim. To use them would have "blown her cover." Hers is an inspiring story of determination and endurance. She wrote several books of which *Magic and Mystery in Tibet* and *My Journey to Lhasa* are again available in English. Her prose is dated, and, even in the 1920's, some of her more extreme claims were contested, but her books are a great read.

Enduring hardship very much like Alexandra's, Heinrich Harrer, too, entered Tibet without permission and traveled for months with a single companion before he reached Lhasa and begged political asylum. Once there, he found first one and then another kind of useful employment and eventually was invited to tutor the young Fourteenth Dalai Lama. He left Lhasa only at the time of the Chinese invasion, in the 1950s.

Col. Austine L. Waddell entered Tibet with what is called the Younghusband Expedition, a force of British soldiers that fought their way to Lhasa in 1904-05 and established a trade mission there which they maintained until the time of the British partition of India. Waddell kept a very detailed journal and published a carefully observed, though not unbiased, book about his journey.

Theos Bernard, the only American to study Buddhism in the monasteries of Central Tibet, was the second American to visit Lhasa. He traveled in 1937 and is now almost unknown. I have had access to his unpublished diaries and letters as well as the reminiscences of his first wife.

As I sort through my stacks of source books, I find Alexandra glaring at me. "You don't like my writing style? You think I exaggerated? What do you know? You're not a student of anything more challenging than basic *hatha* yoga. I could have told so much more...if I'd had a type-writer to keep a diary every night like Theos did, or even notebooks like the Col. Waddell kept. Admitting I could read and write would tell the country people I was a *philang*, a foreigner, and they would have re-ported me to the authorities. I had to carry all my experience in my memory. I can't tell you how amazing I find it to think of you hopping on an airplane in Kathmandu, flying over the Himalayas, looking down on Everest, and arriving in Tibet in a little over an hour."

The other phantoms have joined Alexandra. Theos agrees, "I wish I could have flown in 1947—I wouldn't have been caught in a cross-fire between Muslim and Hindu partisans in the Spiti valley."

Heinrich says to Theos, "We would have met, perhaps climbed a few mountains together. I would have enjoyed that."

"I would have too. If I were still around, I might be as famous as you, Heinrich. A movie might be made about me."

"A dubious honor, but I hoped it would inform more of the public about what has happened in Tibet."

Alexandra gives Theos a fierce look; she now understands why this young man annoyed her immediately. "Heinrich never claimed to be a Buddhist, though I think he has the spirit. YOU obviously learned very little about egolessness in your studies."

Theos, quick to pick up the tone of any situation, responds spitefully, "About as much as you apparently learned, Madam."

Heinrich ignores the spat. He's thinking about mountains, one of his favorite subjects. "Looking down on Everest, imagine!"

ARRIVAL

Momentarily blinded, I held onto the rail as I walked down the steps from the Southwest China airplane and crossed the macadam to the terminal. I blinked back tears from the assault of light. Refreshingly cool air dissolved the claustrophobic cabin closeness. Immediately paradoxes intruded. In the sparkling, modern airport, the luggage X-ray equipment is old-fashioned, unsafe for film. The waiting hall is grand and tastefully decorated, but the bathrooms...pray, God, all bathrooms in Tibet are not like this!

As I quickly escaped the bathroom, Col. Waddell waited, smiling sarcastically. "Welcome to Tibet. That was my first experience too—stink. The disgusting stink of excrement. The town of Phari was our first stop in Tibet, 'the dirtiest place on earth' I called it. Piles of refuse, garbage, excrement, dung inside and outside the houses. Theos, you were in Phari—I don't think the others were—tell her about stink."

"Well, it was a garbage heap, but I was surprised that it wasn't disgusting. In fact, I wrote in my diary..." He shuffled through papers in a leather binder.

"Wasn't disgusting? You're off your rocker, old man. But then, you did

Woman at Gonggar separating grain from chaff

have delusions, didn't you. A reincarnated lama...reincarnation itself— humpffft."

"Here, here, I have it." Theos pulled a typewritten page out of the folder. "Phari, May 19th...dah-dum-dah-dum...ah, here. This was my on-the-spot impression—yes, Colonel, it was filthy. I wrote:

> The way to account for these people being able to continue wallowing in the defiling filth of Phari year in and year out is that their inner souls must be in accord with the rhythm of nature that flows here for in no place on earth have I encountered such a stenchless excrement....The village itself is nothing but a big *Jong* (fort) surrounded by narrow lanes of plastered dung among which the villager fulfills an existence of contentment.[1]

The Colonel stared at Theos, open mouthed for a moment. "You're mad. Simply and very obviously mad."

Heinrich had joined the two. "Colonel, I agree that's a very strange reaction, but perhaps he was suffering altitude sickness."

"No excuse. Most of us were sick as dogs. And nearly frozen by that infernal wind, but, believe me, it was not 'stenchless excrement.' Tibet is the filthiest country on earth—or was in my days here."

"For most of it's history Europe was not any cleaner," Theos asserted.

Heinrich pointed out sensibly, "Furthermore what could the Tibetans do? They couldn't dig pits as you and I would, Colonel, not in that—" he looked out the window at the rocky terrain. "You can barely drive in a tent peg. Should they dump their garbage and excrement into a ravine and poison the water for everyone and everything downstream?"

Shussh-shussh, guys, please. Let me explain a few things while everyone gathers their luggage.

When I signed up for this travel course in Tibet given by the Omega Center, a holistic studies institute, I prepared myself to be surrounded by spacy "seekers." As it turned out, my traveling companions were all in their fifties, had had a measure of success in professional lives and were down to earth—not a crank or crock among us.

BK was our American guide. His expertise was helping travelers "experience the sacred," specifically in Tibet and Bali. Our Tibetan guide, Pemba, was more a facilitator than an educator. We had come to "experience Tibet" not learn facts. A mixed blessing. We did not have to conform to a rigid schedule, we were treated like adults with personal agendas, not school children on a field trip. BK and his young Thai companion, YD, were also highly competent at finding the people who can supply the best van, the best rooms, the best food available. World class luxury doesn't exist in Tibet, nor did we expect it, but any transcendental experiences we had would not result from deprivation, hunger and hardship.

We eight Americans had come to explore. Our reasons for coming were various and mostly amorphous. We had high expectations, romantic ideas, and very few facts about Tibet—we were typical tourists.

"They're a sweet, gentle people," said Denise who spoke often of having done a vision quest, implying this trip was a quest as well.

Felicity, a lawyer, said, "They live peacefully and nonviolently. I want to find out what I can from them to help in my conflict resolution work." Clichés and warm, fuzzy thinking sets my teeth on edge and makes me abrupt and blunt. "Felicity, up until early this century Tibetans' ways of dealing with problems were pretty primitive," I said. "Thieves had their hands cut off, sometimes criminals' eyes were put out." I had read vivid accounts of former Tibetan justice. I thought of Waddell's meeting with a criminal on the streets of Lhasa:

> Amongst the crowd there stood a criminal with his neck in a huge padlocked *cangue*, or wooden collar, looking not a bit ashamed of his uncomfortable manacle, and carrying us back to the days of the stockade in Europe.[2]

About fifty years later, Heinrich Harrer wrote:

Theft and various minor offences are punished with public whipping. A board is slung round the neck of the offender on which his offence is written, and he has to stand for a few days in a sort of pillory. Here again charitable people come and give him food and drink. When highwaymen or robbers are caught they are usually condemned to have a hand or foot cut off. I was horrified to see in what manner wounds so inflicted were sterilised. The limb is plunged into boiling butter and held there....In Lhasa such savage forms of punishment have now been discontinued.[3]

The airport, sixty-five miles from Lhasa, is called Gonggar, after a nearby village. We drove past a few low buildings and stopped to visit Gonggar *Chode*. Passing through an adobe gateway, we entered a court-yard of what looked like a modest country estate with a few stone out-buildings. We had left the twentieth century and entered an earlier age. To the left of the monastery entrance a group of elderly men and women sat in a semi-circle near sacks of barley. One woman, dressed in brown worsted and the multicolored stripped apron of married Tibetan women, her head wrapped in indigo hopsacking, stood in front of the group. She held high a large platter-like basket. As barley spilled from the tipped basket, the wind blew the chaff into a pile and the barley heads fell into another basket at her feet. When I was a child in Indiana my Sunday School book had a picture of people in the Holy Land sep-arating the wheat from the chaff in just this way. I had just arrived in another holy land and the picture had come to life.

This small monastery, which is usually bypassed by tourists was built in 1648 and was once famous for its mural painters. Some remnants of this work still survive. On previous trips to Tibet BK had developed friendships with monks in many of the monasteries to which he takes tourists. At Gonggar Chode young monks gathered around eagerly when they recognized this 42-year-old aging American boy. BK opened his backpack and took out photographs and gave one to a young monk. Others recognized him—the subject of the photograph—before he recognized himself, then a grin blossomed, a chuckle bubbled up. The monk peered at his picture. Others reached for it, but he held it tightly by a corner as if afraid it would disappear into the folds of some other monk's robe. BK passed out a few more photographs. Everyone smiled. Voices were excited but remained soft. Are these their first photographs of themselves? Maybe, because most of the monks and novices are from poor families; cameras are a luxury.

At each monastery this scene was repeated. Many times Tibetans asked us to take their picture although they would never see those snapshots. Why did they ask? What did they want? Did they want to come to America stowed away in the little plastic camera case? Or was it a fascination with the camera itself, a desire to be part of the modern world of gadgets?

Inside Gonggar Chode butter lamps burned before the statue of Buddha. This peculiar scent of burning butter and incense pervades every monastery and shrine. The colonel's experience of excrement is no longer true—a modern improvement. Now the scent of Tibet is the strong, rather rancid scent of liquid fat. It pervades souvenirs brought home and I think it will last for years.

Assembly rooms of monasteries are much alike, square or rectangular and hung extravagantly with *thanka* (sacred scroll paintings usually mounted in brocade) as well as with pennants, valances, prayer flags, and *kathag* (offering scarves). Primary colors are everywhere, especially red and gold. Pillars are painted red and decorated with stenciled designs or wrapped in brocade. The walls are covered with murals, paintings of various forms of the Buddha and of wrathful, protective, blue-skinned deities. We used flashlights to see the paintings because only a little natural light from clerestory windows sifts down through the hangings. Ceilings are flat; arches, vaults and domes are unknown in Tibetan architecture. This is the same architectural style used in ancient Egypt.

Where an altar would be in a Christian church is a statue of the Buddha. In front of the statue are butter lamps (*chome*, in Tibetan), money offerings, seven bowls of water, and very often pictures of the present Dalai Lama, the late Pachen Lama, and perhaps one or two other revered religious leaders. Behind the central altar were shrine rooms that housed the most sacred images. Other shrines containing statues opened off the assembly hall, and also functioned as libraries for sacred books. What looks like so many labeled files against the wall were the *Kengyur* and *Tengyur*—the teachings of Buddha and commentaries on these *sutra*, respectively—bound between painted boards and wrapped in silk like precious gifts. The red squares, indeed, were labels. Each holy book has dozens of volumes.

In the main hall were low rows of benches where the monks sit cross-legged during rituals. Drums and long horns lean against the walls ready to be played. Monks' heavy cloaks and sometimes the lamas' hats lie on benches like crumpled ghosts. BK explained, "They symbolize that their owners are always at prayer, even when busy with other activities."

We wandered through the small monastery, the assembly hall and chapels, up to the second floor and into more shrine rooms. We were even allowed into a dormitory room shared by three young monks. At first they had demurred. "They say it isn't neat," Pemba translated.

Pat and Denise implored, "Tell them we have sons, we know what boys' rooms can be like." The padlocked door was unlocked and we entered a plain room that held three cots, a few garments on hooks, odd socks on the floor, a few boxes, a tin wash basin with dirty water and a wet cloth in it. They explained the rooms are locked so that if something disappears, they know it was misplaced, not stolen. "Good locks make good neighbors," Pemba explained. Mark and I simultaneously say, "Robert Frost."

In the courtyard, I photographed the bright-eyed, curious children who fingered my watch, earrings, and clothing. I pointed to the boys' baseball caps with the English words, "Chicago Bulls, Lucky." When I pronounced the words, they giggled and repeated them. Someone called, "Come! See what we've found!" I left the children and followed others around a corner to where monks were constructing a big prayer wheel.

Near a small building a table was stacked high with sheaves of paper, each covered with printed prayers. Inside, several monks were at work wrapping the papers one by one around the spindle of the prayer wheel. When the entire wheel is packed it will be enclosed in bronze: four feet in diameter, six feet tall. This small building is not a mere workshop but the actual site where monks and peasants will come, circumambulate the wheel, turn it, and send the thousands of prayers inside spinning toward the heavens. Most monasteries have a big prayer wheel like this one; often many small ones stand in rows under porticos, easily turned by anyone walking by. They inspire a childish urge to reach out and set them whirling. Also, throughout Tibet, individuals carry small handheld prayer wheels which they turn clockwise with a movement of the wrist. Instead of prayer wheels, some people walk through the streets carrying prayer beads, fingering them, mumbling *mantras*, often the simple, "*Om mani padme hum.*"

"Psst, psst."

Yes, Alexandra?

"Tell them what it means."

I only know that you wrote it means "a jewel in the lotus," or by implication, "in the lotus, which is the world, exists the precious jewel of Buddha's teaching."

"Right. I'm glad you can quote me accurately. This is a country of prayer, understand that and you will understand the essence of Tibet."

Even now after forty years of Chinese Communism, despite the destruction of thousands of monasteries and the murder of an estimated million people, Tibet remains a land of prayer. Probably more mantra are released skyward from Tibet every day than from all the rest of the world combined.

16

Prayer flags, too, were everywhere. These six-by-six inch squares stamped with prayers often have a picture of a horse in the center. The flags are called "wind horses" and wave casually from tree limbs and hang in courtyards of homes and monasteries. They are often strung on a line like banners in the U.S. that announce the opening of a new gas station or supermarket. They are set into a river bank or in the river itself. Often piles of mani stones—flat stones with the carved or painted prayer, *om mani padme hum*, are clustered around them. Prayer flags also festoon bridges and mark mountain passes. I imagine the rarefied air of Tibet singing and sparkling with prayers. Likewise, I imagine the air of New York City sputtering and sizzling with the static of cellular phones, beepers, and police short wave radios.

I am not good on prayer. None of my reading has suggested an explanation of the origin of a prayer wheel or the idea that written prayer, when enclosed in a drum and rotated, sends out energy, entreaty, praise, and intention. I searched for an intuitive explanation but found myself at an impasse before a mindset and culture bafflingly different from my Western experience. I had been in Tibet less than two hours and already my education and intuition were insufficient to explain a fact of their daily life. As we left Gonggar Chode the threshers connected Tibet and Israel in my thoughts. Israel was a crossroads for Western civilizations and was always part of my sense of history. The books written by my phantom guides painted Tibet as a place so cut off from the West that history had stood still. Yet, difficult as travel was, Tibet was never a sealed time capsule, nor is Tibet a metaphor for a spiritual, newage-ish state of mind.

Like Israel, Tibet now exists partly in Diaspora. Israel in Diaspora remembered that their Temple in Jerusalem was destroyed twice; in Tibet, ninety percent of the monasteries have been razed. This has been the cruelest century for both Tibetans and Jews. But my bent is inclusionist so I also remember the people of Rowanda/Burundi, the Slovaks and Serbs and Croats, the people of Hiroshima and Nagasaki, the Armenians, the Kurds, the gypsies, the Vietnamese, Burmese, Cambodians,

Salvadorans, the Yanomani of the Amazon. For every group facing destruction I have heard of there are probably two more I don't know about. All over the globe this has been, and continues to be, a blood thirsty, terrifying century.

Every traveler wrote of his or her first glimpse of the Potala Palace, standing like a gold crowned guardian angel above the city of Lhasa. I had seen lots of pictures. Finally a moment came when BK said, "Watch to your right, you'll see the Potala in a minute." YES! There it was, far, far away. A castle, red against the milky blue of the sky, the golden roofs a mere glitter in the distance. Nearby trees blocked my view, then it reappeared, disappeared, reappeared, disappeared.

"It's not the same in a van—not at all!" Theos said. "I was so excited!"

I know, I remember what you wrote:

> Eagerly we rode on, so that we might see around a small ridge. Norphel pointed out one could get the first view of the Sacred City, adding that every passer-by always flung a stone on the growing hill as he gazed at the remote goal.
>
> So at a fast gallop we made for this marker, where it was possible to discern our destination through the passing mists of the morning.
>
> At first we could see nothing. Then, suddenly, as the sun rose above the mountain range, a cluster of golden roofs gleamed forth a radiance and a splendor such as I scarcely ever dreamt of. We were now eight miles away and heading straight for this Mirror of the Gods.
>
> The trails were marked with endless rock carvings of Tibetan saints. There was a tremendous image of Buddha carved in the rock facing the Holy City. The houses were rich in their broad stripes of red, white and blue.[4]

But instead of rock carvings and gaily striped houses that Theos described, we entered into urban blight. Hundreds of thousands of Chinese have settled here. Army barracks, and industrial buildings are a disheartening first impression of the long forbidden holy city.

Theos Bernard, in Tibetan robes

FUN-DAY LHASA

"Where will you stay?" Dr. Bernard asked when I said I was planning a trip to Tibet.

"At the Holiday Inn in Lhasa."

"Holiday Inn! In Lhasa?" We laughed.

Dr. Viola Bernard was partly responsible for my curiosity about Tibet. I had worked part time for her for ten years and I had heard her personal history often. She had never been to Tibet, but, as a medical student, she married a man whose ambition was to study Tibetan Buddhism. Viola and Theos Bernard were golden youth in the 1930s. They had intelligence, personal charm, self-confidence, connections, and money. She, an heiress, had the wherewithall to finance an around-the-world trip that included a remarkable diversion for Theos who was writing his doctoral thesis on hatha yoga and hoped to make a reputation for himself as a scholar of Tibetan tantric literature.

After they visited Japan, China, India, and Ceylon, Theos went to study in Sikkim while Viola, who had just earned her M.D., returned to the United States to begin a medical internship. In Sikkim, Theos undertook rigorous hatha yoga training and intensive study of Tibetan, both the spoken language and the very different formal, written language. Going to Lhasa was not part of his original plan but, through a variety of connections and his quick adaptability, he eagerly opened the door to opportunity when it knocked. He was accepted as a serious student of Tibetan Buddhism, even to the point of being told he was a reincarnated lama and initiated at Ganden Monastery by its head, the Tr'i Rinpoche. In 1937, when Theos was in Tibet, the current 14th Dalai Lama had not yet been recognized. Theos reported many meetings with the Regent who was his age.

Except for being in a fenced compound with a guard at the gate, the Holiday Inn looked like any number of American hotels, complete with fountain and roses in the courtyard. It is a joint venture between the Chinese government and the British Forte hotel chain.

Waddell came striding in from the street outside. He had been studying the institutional buildings across the way, each guarded by a Chinese soldier at the gate. The sense of colonial control and orderliness reminded him of India. He felt comfortable, at home. "Well, what a fine wide street, busy too, plenty of traffic. Who would have imagined little Lhasa could become such a bustling city. And clean! That's what I call progress."

Rinchen Dolma appeared beside me. "They're all CHINESE!" she said, a flash of fury in her eyes.

Theos and Heinrich rode in on ponies from the direction of the Norbulinka, the summer residence of the Dalai Lama. The entrance was a quarter of a mile away. They were shaking their heads as Heinrich said, "Well, it's an improvement since '82 when I returned. Look—" He pointed at the sprawl of venders, mostly Tibetan women, on the sidewalk outside the gate of the Holiday Inn. They had spread cloths to display jewelry and trinkets for sale. They wore colorful clothing, including the traditional brightly striped aprons. Some had adorned their hair with strings of artificial turquoise, falsely bright from cheap dye. They wore necklaces of bright beads, bracelets, and earrings—any one of which they would gladly take off and sell to an interested tourist. A few

22

toddlers wandered about on unsteady legs. Some bicycle rickshaw men had parked at the gate, waiting for customers.

"Better buildings, you mean?" Theos asked.

"No, I mean the women's clothing. During the Cultural Revolution even the Tibetans had to wear gray and brown, no bright colors or jewelry. They weren't even allowed to grow flowers in pots—there was to be no beauty except Mao's beliefs. It was a horror, I was sick at heart throughout my return trip."

"Colonization can be a good thing for a backward country," Waddell said. Everyone turned accusing eyes on him, tightened their jaws, pressed their lips into thin, hard lines, and turned away. "Oh, come now. It's a modern city. It wouldn't have happened without the Chinese."

Theos, Heinrich, and Rinchen Dolma spoke as one. "Yes it would have!"

"Modernization was coming, but not like THIS," Rinchen Dolma said forcefully. "We had ideas, things were changing, slowly perhaps but my husband and others—"

"That's right," Theos and Heinrich said. "There were a lot of forward thinking people."

"Change is inevitable," Alexandra sighed. She had joined the group around me as luggage was being unloaded from the van.

"This is not Lhasa—" Rinchen Dolma gestured at the hotel and the buildings across the street. "And is this where visitors stay today? I can hardly tell where I am. It used to be all willow groves and marshes here."

"This is where the wealthy visitors stay. There are other hotels, not so luxurious," Alexandra told her. "If she wanted to stay in a place like this, why didn't she stay home?"

"I understand how you feel, Mary-la," Theos said, taking her hand. "This Holiday Inn looks very grand and I'm sure the rooms are comfortable, but I'd a hundred times rather stay at Tsarong House, or even like you, Alexandra, at a small inn. Nevertheless, in the countryside, I stayed in some dreadful hovels and I can tell you one shouldn't sneer at comfort."

You certainly were comfortable in Lhasa, as was Heinrich during the period he stayed in the same rooms at Tsarong House. Built in 1923, it was the most westernized home in Lhasa.

"If Mary-la doesn't mind, I'll tell you my first impressions of Tsarong House," Theos said.

"Of cousre I don't mind," Rinchen Dolma told him.

"After greetings I was conducted to my suite which was to be my home for a while to come. It revealed my host's thoughtfulness. Not only did it contain Tibetan chairs and tables, but also a desk had been fitted up for me in typical Western fashion. There was a large living room, arranged in regular Tibetan fashion, its supporting beams all handcarved and painted...

"The low cushions upon which I would do most of my work were covered with lovely Tibetan rugs of dragon design. In my living room there was a Buddhist shrine, with the Lama of the house to carry on the chants for me each morning and to bring fresh holy water daily, as well as to keep the Buddha lamp filled so that the eternal light should never go out....I also had a separate bedroom, a toilet with our old-fashioned arrangements, towel racks, portable bathtub, etc., as well as a storeroom for my boxes. Never could I have dreamt of such comfort.[5]

"Yes, that's just as I remember it," Heinrich said.

Alexandra has been listening intently. "Oh, my, what a contrast. I felt lucky when I found a narrow cell in a ramshackled inn occupied by beggarly people."

But it fit your purpose. You maintained your disguise and were able to stay in Lhasa for all the New Year festivities.

"Well, that's true and it was luxury to have my own room, small and dirty as it was, after months of living in the open or begging a bit of floor space in peasants' cottages."

The phantoms, all curious about this huge hotel, followed me into the room I shared with Felicity and Elizabeth. We had arrived at Lhasa's 12,500 foot altitude from Kathmandu which is only about half as high.

"Nearly everyone has some trouble adjusting," BK told us. "You'll find pillows of oxygen in your room. You should use them."

"Just tell me having oxygen available isn't a great step forward," Waddell said to the others.

Rinchen Dolma shrugged. "I remember flying to Peking with a Tibetan delegation that hoped to negotiate with the Chinese. I didn't want to go but they wanted a woman to be included so I could not refuse. In the small airplane, we Tibetans were quite comfortable, but the Chinese crew haggled over a single canister of oxygen, groaning about their splitting headaches, blurry vision, and nausea."

Alexandra gestured, so what? She had never had any difficulty—not with altitude.

Heinrich gave her a smile of agreement, "When you come in by foot as Madame Neel and I did—"

"*David*-Neel."

"Every one of us had headaches, lethargy, and worse—and we walked in too, you know," Waddell said. "The poor buggers who built the roads and carried in the provisions were the worst off; most of them had never been out of the lowlands, never seen snow."

"Poor buggers is right," Alexandra muttered.

Shush-shush, friends. Altitude sickness is a very real problem for today's tourists who fly here and have to adjust to a third less oxygen than at sea level. Altitude sickness is unpredictable, both in terms of who will suffer it and when, as well as what the symptoms will be. On my first trip to Tibet I had no altitude sickness, only a mild headache the evening I arrived. On my return trip I had the classic symptoms, though mildly: lethargy, loss of appetite, headache, and a few hours of fever. Others were not so lucky. Ruth, my roommate on that trip, was very ill for the first five days. Poor Ruth used endless pillows of oxygen and drank gallons of water, trying to avoid dehydration. I came to feel strongly that prophylactic Diamox causes as many problems as it solves. It is a diuretic and necessitates finding a toilet in toiletless places while drinking water by the quart, if not the gallon.

During our first dinner in Lhasa the lights went out. "It happens most nights," BK said. "Sometimes just a flicker, sometimes a few minutes, sometimes maybe half an hour." By the time he had explained, the lights were back on—this time.

Theos wrote that Lhasa had electricity in the early 1930s and was proud of being a modern "electric city" though power supplies were sporadic—far more so than they are now. Even so, Lhasa had electricity before my home in rural Indiana did, for I remember the wiring of our farm house a little before I started school, in the mid-'40s.

During dinner BK gave us no lectures about Lhasa or what we would see, but he offered practical advice, such as if we were out on our own and wanted to return, we should take a bus, taxi, or rickshaw. The address to give was "Fun-day Lhasa." No explanation needed.

THE JOKHANG

At dawn I was awakened as the sound of baritone voices singing in chorus drifted through the open window. Another morning I heard the deep, deep groan of horns like dragons protesting the dawn. Yet another morning trumpets, a reveille. The men's voices, I later discovered, were Chinese soldiers being trucked in from their barracks outside Lhasa for the day. The groaning horns were from the Potala, the trumpets yes, truly a reveille, also the Chinese soldiers. Even with the window open it was not cold, but I enjoyed the cozy wool blanket, the thickest I had ever seen. I expected much cooler weather at this altitude in October until Felicity told me, "Lhasa is at about the same latitude as New Orleans and Cairo."

We began our introduction to Lhasa with a drive through broad, tree-lined streets that have bicycle lanes, past an intersection with a heroic statue of two gold yaks—looking somewhat more intelligent than most of their live counterparts—and past the Potala. Although Lhasa bustled with mini van buses, bicyclists, pedestrians, lorries, and military jeeps, only one corner had enough congestion to require a traffic policeman.

Rinchen Dolma (Mary) Taring, as a young woman

We stopped at the open rectangular area in front of the Jokhang, the oldest and holiest Buddhist shrine in Tibet.

Alexandra came to meet me. She had already circumambulated the Jokhang on the *Barkor*, the market area that surrounds it. "Look at this! Look what they've done!" She bristled with indignation.

What, Alexandra? The square, you mean?

"Square, rectangle, whatever." Her arm swept the open area in front of the Jokhang where rows of venders sold everything from fruits and nuts to prayer flags and blocks for stamping them, and all kinds of trinkets. "It's been Haussmann-ized, just like Paris. The hubris! The unmitigated gall! There was no square here. And those streets your van drove through—new, every one. You didn't think Lhasa was this way when we all saw it, did you?"

Well, actually, I didn't think.

"It's a good thing we're here to tell you to think." Alexandra turned to Rinchen Dolma, "This isn't the Lhasa you and I knew, is it?"

"No, but at least the Jokhang has been returned to us," Rinchen Dolma said.

"Returned—?" Alexandra asked. "What happened?"

"The Chinese used it for storage for several years. There was some destruction, but mostly that's been repaired, I understand. It will always be the holiest place in Tibet. If you'll excuse me, I'm going to buy some incense and butter so I can make offerings."

"I'll come with you. And you —" Alexandra turned to me.

Me?

"Who else? Do your companions hear me?"

No, you're MY ghost.

Alexandra said sternly, like a school teacher determined to teach kindergartners some manners, "You, go in. No, get some incense first. I know you claim you don't pray. So, okay, don't pray, just offer some incense. We are what we do, not what we say." She disappeared into the smoke behind the incense burner, following Rinchen Dolma.

The morning was overcast, the skies were low and the incense smoke hung like a ceiling. Waddell called the Jokhang "the St. Peters of Tibetan Buddhism." But the smoke is not dense enough to hide a St. Peter's or any other European-style cathedral. The Jokhang is, in fact, a three story building of local stone with a plain facade.

BK had bought a bag of incense and gave each of us a handful. When everyone had made an offering, we went beyond the smoke to the small outer courtyard.

"Psst. Psst." Waddell has positioned himself like a tour leader about to deliver important facts. "Allow me to place this building in historical perspective. It was erected in 652 A.D. when Christianity was being introduced into barbarian England, when Mahomet had just died, and when the fanatical Sarcens, having conquered Palestine, were preparing to overrun Europe, before the Middle Ages. The builder was King Srong-sten Gampo —"[6]

Rinchen Dolma, who had been prostrating in the courtyard before entering the building, came over. "Colonel, your sources were Chinese. I want to explain the Jokhang's origins as I learned them from my Tibetan instructors."

"But, Madam, I made a study—"

"I'm sure you did, Sir, but I grew up—" She gestured toward the square, "—not far from here. I learned that the Jokhang was built by the Nepalese Princess, Balsa, who married our King Srongtsen Gampo. When the King asked for the hand of this princess her father commanded her to go to Tibet and as part of her dowry she was given a most precious image of the Lord Buddha, said to have been blessed by himself....Balsa wanted to build a temple in Lhasa for this image so she asked Gyasa—the King's Chinese wife—about a site and was advised to build on a small lake in the city; but as Balsa had a doubt about this she consulted her husband who confirmed, after prayer and meditation, that the lake was the correct site. To fill it up many goats carried loads of earth and stone on their backs....The three storied building was constructed of wood and stone and its wonderful architecture was influenced by ideas from India, China and Tibet.[7]

30

"That's what I put in my memoir. You see, in Tibet, women do not disappear in their husband's shadow. It was Balsa and Gyasa who convinced the King to adopt Buddhism as the religion of all of Tibet. It was only right that Balsa made the decision about building the temple. And Gyasa built the Rimoche monastery for her image of Buddha. You'll visit it too, it's not far away. Thank you for letting me say that."

Thank you, Rinchen Dolma. I like your version better than the ones I've read in other books. Books written by men never give the women credit.

The building we approached was the result of accretions over the centuries but even so has not become very large. The small courtyard was full of people prostrating full length on the stone slabs. Many wore mitts on their hands which made a swish-swish sound. "It used to be much noisier," Waddell said, "an infernal din, in fact. Their mitts were usually studded with nails or even had horseshoes attached to the palm."

Theos added, "Some people brought boards on which to prostrate and would do ten thousand prostrations in a lifetime. Many lay practitioners prostrated a hundred thousand times as part of the *ngondrol*, a foundation for further initiation and spiritual study."

"I never understood religious fanaticism," Waddell muttered, he turned away.

"The opium of the masses, Colonel," Theos said to his back.

Waddell turned quickly and gave Theos a startled look. "I'm surprised to hear you say anything so sensible."

"I forget where I read it, actually. But don't jump to conclusions about me. In fact, like you I find religion as practiced by the masses, here and everywhere, empty and superficial, but these people are striving for perfection in ways their society has taught. It's small of us to be contemptuous of people who are ignorant by chance rather than choice."

"We Westerners can't help bringing our perspective with us." Alexandra, like Waddell, is in a lecturing mood today. "Theos, you and I shared an attitude not so different from Col. Waddell. Here's what I wrote about the Jokhang:

> A strange sight is the crowd of pilgrims perambulating silently in the dark, windowless edifice between these motionless personages, many of which are life size. The yellowish light of the butter lamps adds to the strangeness of the spectacle. From a distance it is sometimes difficult to distinguish the living beings from the host of dummies who receive their homage.
>
> Although the statues are of no artistic interest whatsoever, one receives a deep impression from those many faces, immutably serene, whose gaze seems fixed on some inward object and which tell of a mystic method that establishes the mind in an everlasting calm.
>
> I felt saddened at beholding the procession of worshippers, lost in superstition and exactly following the path that was condemned by the very one whose memory they worship. "Beings led by ignorance, who tramp for fathomless ages the sorrowful road to renewed births and deaths," as the Buddhist Scriptures say.[8]

"At least they're allowed to worship," Rinchen Dolma said. "It gives them comfort that they were denied for years."

"Yes, yes," Alexandra said off hand. She changed the subject. "This is no crowd at all. You should have seen the crush of people at Losar when I was here. Hundreds circumambulated the Barkor, people packed into the Jokhang. It seemed everybody in Tibet had come for the celebration."

"It seemed that way because the streets were so much narrower," Waddell muttered.

Just inside the gateway BK pointed out very old, barely visible murals sequestered behind wire fencing on the walls of the interior courtyard. One or two bare light bulbs gave very little light. Inside the main hall

32

the first sight was a thirty-foot seated image of *Champa*. "Buddha of the future," said Pemba. "*Maitreya* in Sanskrit."

As I looked at the statue, Rinchen Dolma said, "It used to be that people only glanced at Champa on entering. We went around all the ancient shrines first, because Champa has not yet come to dwell on earth. He is the Lord of Love."9

But I took a few minutes to look at the statue which was hung with kathag. Pictures of the Dalai Lama and the Pachen Lama hung on either side—rather, that was true in October of 1995. Nine months later the Dalai Lama's picture had been removed here and everywhere. The Chinese authorities, in one of their arbitrary reversals, had even gone door to door in Lhasa confiscating Dalai Lama pictures from the small shrines that are a part of every Tibetan home. This was a reaction to protests by some lamas who had been promptly jailed. Such business-as-usual repressions by tyrannical governments rarely get into the American press.

A stream of pilgrims moved clockwise around the hall, pushing their way into and out of the many small shrines, each of which house one special venerable statue and a variety of other titulary images. Many pilgrims carry butter, often in plastic bags, and stop at shrines to spoon a little butter into the lamps that burn in front of the statues. People lay yuan bills on the altar. Some pilgrims prostrate at each step of the circumambulation, others prostrate only in front of certain shrines. Often a pilgrim pushes other people aside, gently but quite firmly.

I followed BK and the others into a small chapel; it was close and warm from the many butter lamps and the crush of people. I had no idea what the image represented. I suppose Theos or Rinchen Dolma or Pemba could have told me, but it would have only gone in one ear and out the other. I didn't belong there, making it difficult for the Tibetans to worship as they wished. The scent and heat made me a little nauseated, the gentle pressure of Tibetans pushing past me as they entered and left gave me mild claustrophobia. I slipped out and stood in the aisle.

Waddell approached from the opposite direction in which people were circumambulating. Suddenly Theos stood beside me and stepped in front Waddell.

"You're going the wrong way, Colonel," he said. The colonel gave him a hard stare. "It's customary," Theos explained, as if the Colonel didn't know this fact that could be learned from the most casual observation, "to circumambulate clockwise."

"I KNOW that."

"Then what the bloody hell do you think you're doing?" Theos hissed.

Waddell seemed wary of Theos. He tried a distracting ploy. "Looking for mice," he said with a little smile. "You remember the mice, don't you?"

Theos looked down at the floor, left and right. "Yes. There were hordes of them. I remember that sweetish, musty smell from generations of their nests. Where have they gone?"

"I was wondering that. There's plenty of butter for them. Back there I passed a vat of at least twenty-five gallons. But not a single mouse. It's incredible."

Oh, I think I know.

"YOU know?" Theos and Waddell both seemed to think I was terribly presumptuous to tell my ghost guides anything.

I've read a lot since I first met you guys. Catriona Bass, a British teacher of English, worked here in Lhasa in 1985 and wrote about her experiences. She says that in the so-called Great Leap Forward weekly quotas of pests were imposed."

"What pests?" Theos asked.

Red Guards.

"What!?" Waddell and Theos look at me like I've lost it.

No, of course not. I was joking. If you don't mind a quote from a more modern source—

> ...the "Campaign Against the Four Pests"...was a part of the
> 1958 Great Leap Forward, Mao's disastrous drive to solve

China's economic problems by labour-intensive industriali-sation. Every citizen had to exterminate a weekly quota of birds, flies, rats or mosquitoes. Schoolboys were issued with catapults, the girls with fly-swatters....Once a week they would have to queue up with their jars to prove that they had killed their quota. It was a lengthy process. Each pupil was made to tip his dead flies on to the table and count them out one by one before the class leader. Later when the targets were made impossibly high, they started breeding flies themselves. But no one raised birds, that would have been too difficult. Nor were [the birds] reprieved in Tibet as they were elsewhere in China where the catapillar popula-tion multiplied in their absence. Many species died out alto-gether. There were no doves now, no pigeons, and some varieties of duck had not recovered from the attack on their numbers.[10]

I think we can assume the Jokhang's mice were considered pests and were killed at the same time. This also explains why we saw no pigeons in the square outside.

"Well, perhaps you don't really need us," Theos said, a touch insulted.

"Don't try to tell us we're superfluous." Waddell said. "I drew a de-tailed floor plan of the Jokhang for you. I wrote at considerable length. I told you about those chain curtains blocking the doorway of the shrines. See? There they are, open today. But I don't care if they were closed when I was here. I'm not interested in their idols."

"Would you like me to escort him out?" Theos asked. "I don't think you need him in here."

Yes, please. And take him around the way he came, make him walk clockwise.

Waddell planted his feet firmly apart. "You'll have to drag me."

"I'll help." Heinrich has arrived. He was not a frequenter of shrines and monasteries or an active observer of holy days, but his seven years in Tibet gave him respect for local customs. Theos and Heinrich each took Waddell by an arm and marched him, quickstep, between them, among and over some prostrating Tibetans. After all, they could not see or feel these ghosts of mine.

In an uncrowded moment I went into the shrine with the seventh century statue brought by Balsa, the Jokhang's builder. It is the holiest shrine in this holiest building. The statue seems primitive and not particularly beautiful to me. I agree with Alexandra's aesthetic judgement.

After thoroughly exploring the main hall, we went up the steep stairs to the next level. Here we could walk around a balcony at the level of Champa's head. It was peaceful away from the pilgrims, up near the windows looking down at the thankas and hangings and the placid, long eared, scarf-draped head of the Lord of Love. In one corner a new mural was being painted under bare electric bulbs. The painters, balanced on scaffolds, worked quietly with unselfconscious precision. The colors were bright and primary, garish. Tibet has no Sistine ceilings. Although some early artists were known by name and a few painted themselves among groups of lamas, most art work is communal, anonymous, and traditional as is the fine artesian work that decorates Europe's medieval cathedrals. Except in the Potala, very little early art work has survived the Chinese Communist destruction.

A ladder-like stair led to the roof of the Jokhang. Golden pagoda-shaped roofs gleamed under the gray sky, topping the most holy chapels below in the main hall. The roof was decorated with the stylized pair of deer that are on all Buddhist structures, a reminder that the Buddha's enlightenment occurred at Sarnath, a deer park near Bodhgaya in India. Mythical beasts' heads jut from roof corners like gargoyles on European cathedrals. A few other Westerners were downstairs, but up here we had escaped them as well as the pilgrims. The only Western counterpart I know of is the often visited roof of the Cathedral in Milan, which is a thrilling place to stroll, but it's a tourist site, not a working part of the cathedral. In Tibet monastery roofs are mini-villages where monks live amid small shrines and assembly halls—a semi-private place.

We were only three stories high but central Lhasa spread out below us. Traditionally all houses in Lhasa were lower than the top of the Jokhang because Tibetans considered it disrespectful to look down upon such a holy building. Beyond the haze of incense smoke, the Potala stood majestically on its hill above the city. The Potala, of course, is an exception since it was the home of the god-king. The Chinese are beginning to build seven and ten story buildings—so far only on the outskirts of Lhasa. The feeling for history that inspired the planners of modern Jerusalem to decree that buildings be made of native stone, thus making the city organically part of it's landscape, is certainly missing here.

We heard a drum beating regularly. Like filings to a magnet we were drawn toward the sound. Voices were chanting. In a small, dark assembly room here atop the Jokhang a dozen or so monks sat in two rows, facing the drummer who was in front of a simple shrine. A couple of horn players sat side by side against the back wall. One by one we took places along the wall, sitting cross-legged on the chilly, stone floor. BK, Mark and Sharon immediately took meditation poses.

I sat near the horn players. One followed lines of text with an index finger. He picked up his horn and blew a long note and then a few shorter ones. Almost as an afterthought, the second horn player did the same. He had not been following the page, he did not seem very interested. Their horns are long brass tubes without vents or stops, the prototype of which was made from a human thigh bone. Indeed thigh bone horns are still used throughout the Tibetan-speaking world. When the horn notes climaxed the drummer crashed cymbals several times as if specifically to interrupt the monotony of the chanting, to wake anyone who is dozing or falling into mere rote recitation. The chanting paused, then began again as the drum returned to the steady beat.

I wondered if the indolent horn player had had a bad night and was having a not-any-better day. Or was he one of the monk-spies the

Chinese employ? BK had said that, because rebellion usually is fomented in the monasteries, some Tibetans are enlisted as informers.

The chanting monks are all young men in their twenties or early thirties dressed in thick, maroon-colored robes. They ignored us, for which I was glad. After all, this ritual is meaningful to them and we were not invited. Theos made a great point of his being the first American and only "European" to take part in ceremonies with the lamas. But now apparently tourists can come in and sit down as they wish. But I felt uncomfortable about intruding here and hoped the monks didn't mind our presence.

Admittedly the chanting was hypnotic, the drum beat compelling. Seated around the edges of the small room, my companions looked peaceful. For a moment I imagined Mark was Theos—he seemed to have effortlessly slipped into a peaceful meditation. This introduction to ritual chanting in a small, intimate room atop the Jokhang finally calmed my thoughts and drew me into the rhythm. I put my fingers on my wrist and felt that my pulse was throbbing in time with the drum.

THE POTALA

A hill is to climb. A hill is to build a fort on, or a castle or a palace. Some hills demand human use. In Lhasa, surrounded as it is by high, bare mountains, are two hills, Potala and Chakpori. The latter is smaller in area but slightly taller. It was once surmounted by a medical college. The buildings all the pre-1959 travelers saw on Chakpori Hill are gone, a monument to the awful nature of invasion and the will to destroy a people's culture, not even respecting medicine, the most humane pursuit. Chakpori Hill is now topped with a tall antenna which helps our TVs at the Lhasa Holiday Inn receive dopey '50s Batman episodes.

Heinrich was at my side as our van took us to the Potala. "Not only Chakpori but much, much else has been obliterated," he told me. "I was shocked when I returned in 1982. I saw prayer-flags flying on top of Chakpori, but they were flying over ruins...the medical school on the summit of that mountain was destroyed at the time of the 1959 rebellion—not by Red Guards. Nor did I see the five great *chorten* of Bardogalin at the western entrance to the city, which had been the doorway to a new life for us ragged fugitives many years ago....The western gate was another monument destroyed even before the cultural revolution in

The golden roofs over the Dalai Lama's tombs

order to make a huge highway. It stood between the Potala and Chakpori...I recalled massive stupas, the central three linked by ropes from which hung dozens of little bells which emitted a silvery note in the slightest breeze. In spite of the arid climate the stupas had a marvelous patina and were overgrown with moss. The explanation of this unusual feature in the dry Tibetan highlands were the numerous tiny rivulets which ran everywhere in those old days."

My goodness, Heinrich, I only see those two stupas.

"It is totally changed...a little pond lay to the west of the city gate, and stupas were reflected in its surface. On the water of the pool, masses of colourful ducks and other migrating birds would scurry about...Later after I had been living in Lhasa for some time, two more stupas were erected."

Rinchen Dolma had joined us. She said, "Now all five of them have been destroyed, and the legend that used to be told in Lhasa has become sad reality. According to this legend the Potala and Chakpori were the head and tail of a dragon, whose body linked the two hills. When the dragon's body was pierced in order to build the city gate there had been great anxiety among the people, for the legend predicted a disaster for Lhasa if the dragon's body were wounded, and, in order to avert that, the dragon's 'spinal vertebra' was repaired by means of these great stupas, which were to protect the capital against future misfortunes. Now they have all been destroyed, and disaster has certainly befallen the city."[11]

"It's remarkable the Potala wasn't destroyed," Heinrich said.

"Yes. My husband reported seeing the Potala hit by shelling as he fled Lhasa as part of the Dalai Lama's retinue," Rinchen Dolma said.

The palace was saved from destruction by a direct order from Chou En Lai who declared it a precious historical monument—a fact I read several times.

No longer in a setting of fields and meadows that once greeted travelers, ugly housing blocks have been thrown up, tenements for Lhasa natives whose homes were razed to make way for urban "improvements." The Potala Palace grows out of the hill on which it sits, organically rising out of the stone, it's impossible to tell where the hill ends and the palace begins. Once, the Potala Palace was the tallest building in the world, which it remained until the Eiffel Tower was built two centuries later. Construction began about 650 A.D. by King Srongsten Gampo, the same king who made Buddhism the official religion thanks to his two wives. He is responsible for the red portion that forms the heart of the complex. A statue of Srongsten Gampo in the Potala showed a dapper man of thirty or forty-something with a pencil-thin cat's whiskery double mustache, an elegant nose, and eyebrows lifted in curiosity. He sits between his Chinese and Nepalese wives, both blandly pretty.

The majority of the palace was built by the "Great Fifth" Dalai Lama, (1617-1682) whose reputation still outshines that of all those who followed him except, perhaps, the present, 14th Dalai Lama. Tibet had devolved into a group of warring provinces, much like Europe was about the same time. With assistance from Mongol allies, Srongsten Gampo decisively defeated the Shigatse Tsang kings and united central Tibet.

A thousand years and much turmoil later in 1642, the Fifth Dalai Lama established his capital in Lhasa. He understood that a grand palace cum monastery would be an important symbol of permanence and unity. The palace was built around the ruins of Srongsten Gampo's palace. Waddell explained the name:

> [The palace's] hill is called "Potala" after the name of a rocky hill overlooking the harbour at Cape Komorin, on the extreme tip of the Indian continent, which the Indians fancied was the end of the world, and on which was placed the mythical abode of the Buddhist God of Mercy, which the Lamas identified with the Compassionate Spirit of the Mountains [Chenresig in Tibetan, Avalokhesvara in Sanskrit] that the Dalai Lama alleged had become incarnate in himself.[12]

The Great Fifth's kingship came about through Tibet's associations with the dynasty of Ghengis Khan. The Mongols never invaded central Tibet. Crossing the Takla Makan desert and forbidding Changthang plains between Mongolia and Lhasa may have been just too much trouble for too little reward compared to the rich Silk Road trade centers. At the death in 1655 of Grushi Khan, the last of the powerful Mongol warlords, Tibet was a newly unified country, vulnerable to invasion. The Tibetans appealed to the Mongols for protection from the Chinese on their northern and eastern borders and the Mongols not only helped but made Tibetan lamas the religious tutors of their scions. Thus a mutually beneficial relationship began that continued into the beginning of this century.

The construction of the Potala as it exists today was not completed when the Great Fifth died in 1682. His Prime Minister, to maintain the status quo and finish the building project, let it be known that the Dalai Lama was retiring from public life, keeping his death a secret. Work continued until the Potala was finished in 1696. Only then did the Prime Minister reveal that the Great Fifth had been dead for fourteen years.

His successor had been found and secretly trained. However something seems to have gone amiss, for the Sixth never took final vows. He built a summer palace called Norbulinka a few miles away. It was surrounded by gardens where he spent a great deal of time with a harem to whom he wrote love poetry. He wrote, in fact, that he had never slept alone; but his defenders suggest that he practiced Tantric yoga (which includes sexual congress). The Sixth's very human weakness endeared him to the Tibetan people who still quote his love poems just as Europeans quote Solomon's psalms praising women's beauty.

As I got out of the van and walked toward the gate of a side entrance where tourists have to enter the Potala, Waddell was waiting for me. "I see you find me quotable on the name."

You researched such things very thoroughly, Colonel. I respect you for that, if not for the condensation toward Indians beliefs. I remember you were very impressed with Lhasa and the Potala. You wrote about your arrival in the Lhasa valley.

43

Here at last was the object of our dreams!—the long-sought, mysterious Hermit City, the Rome of Central Asia, with the residence of its famous priest-god and it did not disappoint us! The natural beauty of its site, in a temperate climate and fertile mountain-girt plain, with the roofs of its palatial monasteries, temples and mansions peeking above groves of great trees, to some extent explains why the Lamas were so jealous of intruders and fits Lhasa, when once its natural and artificial difficulties of approach have been removed, to be one of the most delightful residential places in the world.

The most superb feature of all, undoubted, was the majestic castle of Buddha's vice-regent on earth, which far exceeded the highest expectations we had formed of it. From first to last, from far and near, this imposing pile on Potala hill dominates the landscape and catches and holds the eye.

...The vista which then flashes up before the eyes is a vast and entrancing panorama—about 300 feet high—from top to bottom with its terraces of many-storeyed and many-windowed houses and buttressed masonry battlements and retaining walls, many of them 60 feet high and forming a stately architectural proportion on the most picturesque of craggy sites.[13]

You were quite taken with it, Colonel. I get the feeling imperial architecture stirs your heart.

"And why not? What is noble in us responses to what is noble in the world. The Potala Palace is a noble building."

Theos had joined Waddell and me at the wooden door which is decorated with brass fittings and a yak's tail as a pull cord.

"It's rather unceremonious to come in the back way, don't you think?" Theos asked. "I never did."

"Nor, I," Waddell said.

"YOU were here only once, Colonel."

"I suppose you were here many times."

"Yes. I was shown shrines no other Westerner had ever seen—perhaps has not seen to this day."

"Well, we didn't come to look at shrines. We came to strike a treaty with the government. We were concerned about the safety of our India, not about golden idols."

I believe Gen. McDonald and Col. Younghusband were concerned about their own safety, weren't they? Most of your force remained in full battle readiness down there.

"We had no idea if we were walking into an ambush. It was a damned ticklish situation, I can tell you. Narrow, dark corridors, tall staircases. Made the hair at the back of my neck stand up, I don't mind admitting."

Did you leave specific orders for them to rescue you after a certain amount of time? I couldn't help wondering as I read your book.

"The military secrets of the British Army are not for me to disclose. We would have been irresponsible to enter an enemy fortress without precautions."

"Enemy!" Alexandra exclaimed. "Does a government become your enemy because they won't answer your letters?"

"Madam, your views are highly biased and this is hardly the occasion on which to educate you about the reason for our mission to Lhasa."

Alexandra stared daggers at Waddell for a few moments then turned to me. "Do you mind if I come along? I only managed to come in with the Losar crowd. So much to see but I saw so little. Being short and small the throngs pushed me along much too fast." Alexandra sighed regretfully.

Of course, you're very welcome, Alexandra.

Theos said rather smuggly, "I saw it all and photographed all I could. It's too bad I was never able to publish most of my photographs. Of course I ruined a lot of film in bad light—but I was allowed to photograph shrines and ceremonies no one had ever photographed, shrines that are gone now, ceremonies that can no longer be conducted because those who understood them are dead. My record was invaluable."

"Well, you didn't take proper care of it. So it's gone." Waddell snapped. "And if the others are too polite to mention it, I'll do it for them—this incessant braggadocio is downright unbecoming, very irritating, and certainly bad manners."

"It's not braggadocio, it's fact. And if I don't mention it no one will know. I was not traveling with half an army—or even with eight 'seekers.' I was alone! Only I know what I saw and did. The world has forgotten me." Theos stopped, a little embarrassed as he heard the petulance in his own voice.

Shussh-shussh! I'm as eager to see the Potala's interior as you were.

Formerly the center of a theocracy, with both secular and religion leaders bustling about, running the country, the Potala is now a museum, empty except for its monk guards and very few tourists. Soon we were walking through a corridor-like room that is a depository for hundreds of volumes of *Kangyur* and *Tengyur*—many times as many in this one corridor than we had seen in little Gonggar Chode. The shelves began about four feet from the floor and extended to the dim heights of the ceiling. We followed the ritual of stooping and walking under the books, it's said to help one understand their messages. I saw some pilgrim women hold their infants under shelves of books as they mumbled prayers. I wondered if the mothers hoped the babies would become lamas.

The Great Fifth's tomb is the grandest in the Potala which contains tombs of all the succeeding Dalai Lamas (several of whom died as young men, possibly murdered by powerful regents who were reluctant to give up their power, or who, some writers suggest, were in collusion with the Chinese). To me the Great Fifth's tomb did not look remarkably different from many other shrines, though a great deal of gold was used to gild it and its bas relief embellishments are studded with jewels which are cabachon cut rather than faceted.

"Psst-psst." Theos was beside me.

I know, Theos, you attended a ceremony here at the Great Fifth's tomb. And your book has a wonderful photograph of it. The lamas are wearing splendid, complex hats.

"I wasn't going to say that. Anyway, their hats were the least of the wonders. Walking these empty halls, you can't begin to imagine the pomp and ceremony that once filled these rooms."

"Speaking of hats," Alexandra said and began to chuckle. "Can I share with the others my hat problem that nearly, as you would say, blew my cover here at the Potala?"

Why don't you tell it yourself?

"Gladly. I'm sure everyone remembers that I was in disguise. Yongden and I wanted to see the Potala, of course, but we wanted to have a cover story, you might say. So he told a couple of countrymen he would act as their guide. They felt honored to have a lama to explain the statues to them. And, of course, I tagged along. We climbed up the steps and the men entered first. I was about to follow humbly, when a...novice lama, short and fat with a red face, flat nose and large ears, looking like a gnome in a clerical robe twice too large for him, stopped me. He was acting as doorkeeper, and he ordered me rudely to take off my fur-lined bonnet, such headgear not being allowed inside the Potala.

What a calamity!...I had worn it a long time...it screened my face and I felt protected against detection when I had it on my head. What now? My hair had resumed its natural brown shade. The Chinese ink I used as a dye had worn away before I reached Lhasa and in my present dwelling, with the cracks in its doors and walls, through which my neighbours could peep at any time, I had not dared to darken it afresh. It no longer matched the braids of jet black yak hair that I wore, and the latter had gradually lost a large part of their substance, until they had become as thin as rats' tails. They were all right, however, with the bonnet on. They shadowed my forehead enough to reproduce vaguely the hairdress of some *dokpa* tribe."

Alexandra paused, shaking her head and smiling at the memory.

"I had to obey that horrid little toad and take my bonnet off, I knew that I should look funnier than any clown in any circus in the world. However escape was impossible. I had my bonnet under my dress, as I was ordered to do, and rejoined my companions. Yongden had lingered a little, waiting for me. At first glance, stricken with terror, he opened his mouth wide and hardly suppressed an exclamation. 'You look like a demon,' he said, trembling. 'I never saw such a funny face in my life! Everyone will stare at you'"[14]

But you say no one looked at your "extraordinary head," I reminded her.

"That's right. The lighting was not good and everyone was intent on the sights in the Potala. I was here for a few hours, in fact, and only when I left I heard one pilgrim ask his fellow, "Where do you think she came from?" Then he answered himself, "She must be a Ladaki."

The two oldest shrines in the Potala are also the holiest and contain very ancient statues. They are entered after going through many passageways and many other shrines and they seem like grottos hewn from the bedrock of the palace. No other tourists were there so our group stood in a circle silently holding hands for some time. These two rooms are so deep in the interior of this enormous building that if it were a human body they would be the right and left chambers of the heart.

I found the wall paintings—and all walls seemed to have been painted—more fascinating than the tombs and shrines. Future generations of scholars may be kept busy for years cataloging the miniature scenes that cover hundreds of walls. They show the history of the world, the life of Buddha, the history of Buddhism in Tibet, the lives of the Dalai Lamas, also scenes of the construction of the Potala and the Jokhang, scenes of every day life and much else. Exquisite and intricately detailed, in some murals the faces are individualized, expressions and emotions marked.

In a mural of Buddha's life story, I pointed out to BK a picture of an ox cart. "Look! They've painted wheeled carts on their walls but they didn't use wheeled vehicles at all until after the British invasion."

"I didn't know that," BK answered.

"Not invasion, mission," Waddell said emphatically.

I'll argue with you about that later, Colonel. We're talking about wheels now. I hate that colonial euphemism—"mission"—and certainly plan to say more about it when we get to Gyantse.

But Waddell continued. "We had to build roads as we progressed, that's why the mission took six months. Of course we had to have carts. The logistics of supplies was quite a feat. We had a lot of men and animals to feed."

"You should have stayed home," Alexandra muttered, but she said aloud, pointedly, "This is not the time or place to go into that, Colonel."

"Well, the traders managed to haul out a lot of wool and bring in a lot of Indian and Chinese goods using only yaks and donkeys," Theos said. "They had sufficient roads for their needs."

Ignoring Theos, Waddell went on, "There was one wheeled vehicle, a carriage the King of Nepal had sent to the Dalai Lama. It was dismantled and carried, all in pieces on yak back, I suppose. Then reassembled here. They never drove it, just kept it in the Potala — it's probably still here in some forgotten room."

It would be fun to come upon it.

But, of course, there's no chance of coming upon it; we were only allowed to see a few shrine rooms. Ribbons blocked forbidden passages, doorways and stairs while monk-caretakers stood guard in each room. The monks shuffled about with cloths under their feet removing the visitors' invisible footprints.

Some rooms of the Dalai Lama's private quarters were open. The apartment remains as he left it. Although the Potala is enormous, the Dalai Lama's private rooms seemed small, more cozy than grand, certainly compared to rooms in European palaces like Versailles or Windsor Castle. I felt certain that this is His Holiness's real home. A fluke of history had allowed us to wander here in the echoing rooms.

At last we reached the Potala's roof. It reminds me of a giant version of those children's playgrounds that are built with many levels for climbing on, for playing all kinds of hide-and-seek and exploration games. The roof is a grand expanse of many levels, the pagoda-shaped roofs of gold that can be seen from so far away cover the several Dalai Lamas' tombs. They protrude as if the holiness within were so great it bursts in a golden thrust right up through the palace.

The sun was trying to break through thin clouds, the roofs gleamed as did a dazzling array of structures, some drum shaped, many heads of snow lions, dragons, and garudas. Little bells hung from eaves. Windows were covered by white canvas valances decorated with an eternal knot in black applique. We wandered around the roof for a long time, taking pictures, looking at the valley below.

Waddell stood at the edge of the roof looking out. "I would never have imagined it could change so..." he mused.

I liked your description, Colonel. May I quote it?

For the first time, Waddell smiled with sincere pleasure. (A little compliment softens even apparently atrophied hearts.)

He wrote lyrically about this view:

> In this restful panorama, a vast bird's-eye view of the valley of Lhasa and its noble hills, scarcely a hum from the life below breaks upon the stillness. The plain stretches out as a great land-locked sea, with wavelets of green copses, amongst which peep, like ships cosily at anchor on its bosom, the tops of the "cathedral," the town houses, and the cottages beyond with their smoke curling to the sky, and from its green borders purple caps and promontories shoot boldly up into the dark blue snow-streaked peaks fading away into soft azure in the distance.[15]

To my eyes, accustomed to the glass and steel of New York City, the valley remained restful and very beautiful, near and far. The green copses were very distant now, below us a city sprawls; plain, uninteresting block housing has replaced the cottages. Where a park-like meadow and streams were immediately below the front of the Potala there was now a great open square of concrete—more Haussmann-izing. The square is one of Lhasa's newest urban features, constructed for the fortieth anniversary of the "liberation" which was celebrated in May 1995 with a show of military force.

Beyond the valley, nestled in clefts between mountains and many miles apart, were two great monasteries we would visit, Drepung to the west and Sera to the east. They were cities more populous than Lhasa itself in the days when this was a valley full of cottages and Tibet was a land of lamas.

Alexandra and Rinchen Dolma joined me studying the valley. "Oh, my. I wish I could have seen this," Alexandra sighed.

"I never saw it either," Rinchen Dolma said, "I was always down there, looking up. Only officials came here. And now anyone can—yet your group are the only people up here."

I noticed Heinrich standing near the edge of the roof looking out over the city. Theos was beside him; both had looks of contentment and contemplation. "I spent several nights in the Potala," Heinrich said quietly.

"You did? How come?" Theos asked, surprised, maybe a little jealous.

"With friends, officials, lamas..." For a moment Theos gave Heinrich a long, considering look, but he arrived at no conclusions. "I was helping to build a garden."

"I had a very thorough tour," Theos said, chastened, trying to keep any bragging out of his voice. "The kitchens were the biggest, blackest, hottest places I could imagine, with sooty, greasy cooks hauling about carcasses of meat, huge containers and spoons like canoe oars. If someone had told me I'd died and gone to hell, I would have believed it. But then I was shown the dungeon where prisoners were shackled, hopelessly waiting for death, forgotten by the outside world—or so they felt. And that was truly living hell."

"The place was as complex as an oriental government can be," Heinrich said. "Sanctity and sadistic torture..." He sighed a philosophical sigh.

"I'm glad they preserved the treasures, but it's so empty today—a body without a soul." Theos shook his head.

"It was a kind of prison, I always thought, for little Kundun—"

"You called the Dalai Lama that? Kundun, meaning Presence?"

"Those of us close to him did. He was a small boy, given religious instructions hour upon hour. His only playmate was his older brother, a reincarnated lamas too, you know. The lamas who were his personal servants loved him—I could see it in their faces. Yet he must have been so...Ach! What do we know? Maybe loneliness is something we construct out of jealousy for others who seem to have more love than we. He was both loved and revered, certainly never alone. But he told me he used to bring a telescope up here to the roof to see what life was like in the town. The common people were as exotic to him as he was wonderful to them. It didn't seem to make him sad, but it made me sad for him."

"A boy locked up, even here....He must have wanted to sneak away. I would have," Theos said.

"I couldn't have lived my boyhood without sports, but I was just an ordinary kid living a normal life."

That was long ago, Heinrich. Your life has been anything but normal.

"I've been extraordinarily fortunate in some ways—and the stroke of fortune that has been most rewarding is to have known Kundun when he was a boy and to have helped him learn English and explore Western science and mechanics. I've been allowed to make a meaningful contribution to the life of an extraordinary person."

Reading the description of your experiences was the first time I felt that the Dalai Lama is a real, and very extraordinary person. I don't trust hagiography. But you simply told your story and I admired you both very much.

I do believe Heinrich blushed. "Danke," he said quietly.

Our van was waiting in front now. We walked down the switchbacked grand stairs, noticing wildflowers blooming in straggling bunches along the way. Theos walked at my side, still explaining, "The Thirteenth Dalai Lama loved flowers. He had all sorts planted at Norbulinka. Tibetans in general love color, and the purity of flower colors especially. It's hard to believe even the Chinese could have destroyed flowers in Lhasa.

The Cultural Revolution was a spasm of barbarity. Destroying flowers was the least of it. The Red Guards were boy soldiers, and today there are boy soldiers acting just as cruelly in parts of Africa, probably in other parts of the world as well. Children should not be turned loose with guns, whether they're soldiers, street gangs or American school boys. Theos, you worked in Arizona with the Native Americans—

"For the Bureau of Indians, one summer, yes."

You saw what we did to that culture. The reservations, the poverty, the second class citizenship, apathy toward ancient forms of ritual. It's happening here, colonization, destruction of a culture.

"We didn't think about such things back in the '30s," Theos said thoughtfully. "The world seems to be changing, becoming more aware of the validity and value of other cultures."

I hope so.

I was haunted by the Potala's emptiness, the dark echoing rooms and corridors and their hundreds of unseen counterparts, the eerie quiet of a palace once chockful of busy monks and important comings and goings. Ruined castles of Europe that I have visited were built by warrior princes who lived by the sword and fell by the sword. This palace was the seat of a government whose tragic flaw was the desire to mind their own business, to ignore the world beyond their borders, and, as far as possible, to stop time.

Tibetan woman turning prayer wheels

CHAKPORI HILL

On the way back to our hotel, after visiting the Potala, we drove through an area of unattractive industrial buildings and turned down an unpaved track passing rubble and junk strewn open spaces. We finally came to a ticket booth beyond which was a path that led to the "Blue Medicine Buddha." The large Buddha image and the many smaller ones are sculpted in low bas relief and brightly painted on a rock wall at the base of Chakpori Hill.

Theos and Waddell were pacing back and forth, actually in step with one another, muttering, "I'd never know … I'd be lost … It's entirely different. Hard to believe …" When Theos saw I had arrived he hurried over, "Do you remember the picture in my book?"

The one with the path among trees and grass with wild flowers? Yes, I remember.

"It was a beautiful summer day with high up scattered clouds. I remember a fine, refreshing breeze. This was bucolic countryside. The pilgrim's path wound round the hill."

Waddell said, "I took a color photograph. The wall of Buddha images was vibrantly painted."

"So did I," Theos said. Theos turned to Waddell with an incredulous look. "You had color film in 1905, Colonel?"

"Yes, indeed I did. A small supply. I used it judiciously. And I must say, that photograph turned out quite well."

"The wall was very impressive—so were the medical colleges on top of the hill," Theos said. He turned to me, "Come look at the wall. At least they haven't blasted it away, though the hill's quite a different shape now."

As we looked at the rocky rubble, Waddell explained, "Chakpori means iron hill. Not that it was iron, but it seemed as adamantine as iron, I suppose. It was so picturesque, I did a drawing of the hill crowned with the college buildings.

Yes, it's in your book, it's quite a dramatic drawing.[16] Your description of the hill is worth sharing:

> The Temple of Medicine, as seen from the north, crowns the summit of a high rocky pinnacle, the further side of which sweeps almost sheer down to the river that laps its base; and here on the river bank face the great limestone cliff is covered all over with thousands of brilliantly painted rock-sculptures of Buddhas and other divinities, forming a marvelous piece of varied colour....This striking picture-gallery of coloured bas-relief was evidently begun by the first Grand Lama, Lobzang, as it bears an inscription of his in its centre, and it is still being added to. A scaffolding was to be seen at one end where new images were being chiselled out of the rock. A painter resides in a hut below, who is constantly engaged in keeping the colours in repair.[17]

"It would be interesting to compare our photographs, Colonel," Theos said.

In fact I have compared the two published photographs, which, unfortunately are only in black and white. I cannot feel totally certain

56

they are the same wall. Each shows only a portion and even the large figures of Buddha among the smaller figures do not look exactly the same. We had arrived at the wall and, now that I was confronted with the same structure, it looked somewhat more like Waddell's photograph. I wondered if Theos had photographed a different area. The colors were faded and the paint was flaking off. Certainly no one lives on the premises to keep it well repaired. I could not see the plaque which is clear in Waddell's photo, but his information makes this exuberant wall of images five hundred years old. How strange it was to discover a complex, venerable work of art in the middle of an industrial wasteland.

The variousness of the few pilgrims there told me that the wall still speaks to a cross section of people. Three young women in traditional long skirts and striped aprons did prostrations, a couple of young women in modern slacks stood pressing their foreheads to the wall. A gray-haired woman and a pair of middle-aged men turned the prayer wheels which are in a row in front of the wall, sheltered by a roof. These prayer wheels have been added, I think, since Waddell was here.

Theos and Waddell have taken seats on a stone wall. "You're a medical doctor, aren't you, Colonel?" Theos asked.

"Yes, of course. I was the Chief Medical Officer with the Younghusband Expedition."

"What did you think of Tibetan medical practices?"

"Very primitive, based on feeling pulses. As I wrote, both the sick and the medical lamas themselves relied more on prayer than pharmacopoeia for recovery. In fact, I enquired especially about the treatment for small pox, as it is one of the most deadly diseases in Tibet. Although the Chinese doctors in Lhasa employed inoculation for its prevention, the Tibetans trusted to camphor and a few other aromatics and charms and the priest wound up his account by saying, 'and doing so you never get small pox.'[18]

"However, that same lama admitted the young Dalai Lama had nearly died of small pox and had many pox marks as a result," Waddell said with the sarcasm that the British do so well. "So, you see, the state of medicine was very unscientific." He went on, "I was told the medical course lasted eight years but even if students did not pass their exams they remained at the college here—rather up there, where that—what do you call that metal structure stuck up there?"

It's a television antenna.

"A what?"

I'll explain later. You're very dismissive about Tibetan medicine, but their diagnostic ability and their herbal medications are still esteemed.

"Oh, come, come! They actually told me that women's hearts were in the center of the chest and men's on the left. That the red blood circulated only on the right side of the body while yellow bile flowed on the left."

Well, perhaps that's what they told you back then, but I must tell you that a Tibetan doctor is available to visitors at the Holiday Inn at appointed hours and the members of my group found his prescriptions helpful.

"A bunch of hysterical women, no doubt," Waddell said.

Indeed not! Both men and women saw him and I can assure you most are what our present day media call educated consumers. BK told us the Tibetan medicines seem to relieve altitude sickness as effectively as Western medicines. "Mere palliation, no doubt," Waddell said sniffily.

My guess is the placebo effect had a great deal to do with it. But I will tell you that one person in my first group was accurately diagnosed as having a bowel complaint. She had not given the doctor any medical history beforehand. He gave her herbal tablets and she found so much relief that when I told her I was returning several months later, she asked me to get her another supply of the medicine. She said her relief has been cumulative and she thought she would be symptom-free after a few more weeks of medication.

"Well, you know, of course, that anecdotal reports abound in medicine and finally prove only that something worked for one patient," Waddell said in a lecturing tone. "You cannot make gross extrapolations from a single instance."

Heinrich has arrived from the path that leads some distance up the shattered mountain. "May I add a bit while you're talking about herbal remedies."

Yes, Heinrich, you had more time to observe Tibetan medicine than either Theos or the colonel.

"That's right. I described the herb gathering and preparation."

In the autumn the whole school goes off to search for herbs in the mountains. The boys enjoy the expedition tremendously, though they are kept very busy. Every day they camp in a fresh place and at the end of their excursion they drive their heavily laden yaks to Tra Yerpa. This is one of the holiest places in Tibet. It contains a sort of temple in which these herbs are sorted and laid out to dry. In winter the youngest of these little monks have to grind the dried herbs into powders, which are kept in carefully labelled air-tight leather bags by the abbot in charge of the school....The Tibetans are really advanced in the knowledge of herbs and their healing properties, and I have often had recourse to them. Their pills did not do my sciatica much good, but I staved off many a cold and fever with their herb-teas.[19]

So, Col. Waddell, we have a first hand report.

"Another anecdote," Waddell muttered. "If our profession relied entirely on anecdotes, we would have miracles not medical science."

Colonel, today a serious research society is hard at work seeking herbal knowledge from various indigenous people in the hope of discovering plants with healing properties that have been used for hundreds of years. The emphasis is largely on the rain forests because both the people and the ecosystems are endangered. However I'd suggest that Tibetan herbal knowledge would be a worthwhile subject for attention. The doctor is still dispensing herbal remedies so the lore obviously isn't entirely lost yet.

Waddell cleared his throat, ready to refute me.

Heinrich said firmly, "Don't argue, Waddell. Even if it were only relief for cold sufferers..."

"But who knows?" Theos added, "From the perspective of a man who came to Tibet seeking ancient knowledge, I would agree that valuable information can yet be unearthed."

DREPUNG

Drepung, once the largest monastery in the world, was formerly several miles beyond Lhasa. Now the Chinese settlement on the western side of the city sprawls nearly to it's entrance. We approached through a tree lined lane as Theos said he had. In the parking area we faced a flight of stone steps.

BK's words to the wise were, "Walk up slowly and don't pet the dogs. They've been known to bite people." The dogs were simply inhabitants of the monastery, not watch dogs or pets. Felicity's guidebook related a superstition that if monks and lamas don't live up to their principles they are reincarnated as dogs. These dogs were all scruffy mutts, though they seemed reasonably well fed. Theos reported sixty years ago a dog's life was truly miserable in Tibet. Only the mastiff guard dogs that were kept chained at gateways were cared for.

Theos' *Penthouse of the Gods* includes two impressive photographs of Drepung: one of the monastery from a distance, a white city climbing up a cleft in the mountains; the other of a terrace where lamas sit at daybreak as mist hovers in the valley below. He wrote:

Very young monks, greeting visitors

This immense Buddhist monastery is situated in the upper part of a deep nullah, among great masses of tumbled-down boulders of sandstone...its name, Drepung, means a pile of rice...Its three and four stories of whitewashed dormitories give it the appearance of a pile of auspicious rice—this is if you see it from a proper distance....While the official number of monks housed in Drepung is 7700...these numbers are mythical rather than factual; the real figures...exceed those given by thousands.

It was a hard pull from the great stone entrance to the large rock paved assembly grounds in front of the main temple, where all the monks of four colleges which make up the monastery had gathered for this mass. With each step we ascended another few inches. The buildings were all very close together, leaving canyons wide enough for two persons to walk abreast or a single pack-donkey.

The monastery was erected by Geshe Rabsen-age Gyal-Ts'ab-je in 1414. The final ascent to the Central Cathedral with its glittering golden roof, which can be seen for miles from the surrounding countryside, was a steep, rapidly rising ascent.[20]

"Thank you for letting me introduce this extraordinary monastery." Theos had come along in his brocade chubba.

"I never understood you blokes who go native," Waddell sniffed. He was stiff in his uniform. "Seems to me there's something unstable about people who can't be true their background."

"Not at all, Colonel," Theos answered quickly. "The truth is I had no choice. I had not expected to be away from Sikkim for several months and the riding britches I brought along simply gave out. I had the local tailors fit me out with a new wardrobe."

"They could have made britches for you."

"Perhaps, but I'm sure YOU have never spent hours sitting cross-legged at low tables on pillows or the bare floor. Believe me, these robes are very convenient and comfortable."

I think you look just fine Theos, although I prefer the pictures of you without a beard. However, the readers don't know much about you yet so I'll pause to tell them how you came to be here at Drepung.

"It's high time you did. They probably think I'm fiction."

When Theos Bernard traveled to India and Sikkim in 1936 he knew Lhasa was forbidden to travelers. In 1916 Alexandra David-Neel asked no one's permission but simply hired guides and pack animals and left Lachen, Sikkim, where she was studying and went to Shigatse where she was allowed to study at the Tashilungpo Monastery. When she returned she found the British had fined the people of Lachen heavily for letting her go into Tibet.

Theos knew that Guisseppi Tucci, the well-known and well-funded Italian Orientalist, had been allowed only to go to Gyantse or Shigatse. Seydam Cutting of the New York Museum of Natural History had visited Lhasa briefly in 1934, but he had been more interested in geography and culture than Tibetan religion. Theos' goal was to witness the practices of Tibetan Buddhism and to purchase the ancient Buddhist Tantric texts said to exist only in Tibet's monasteries. Both his father and his uncle were serious, but not academic, Tantric scholars. Theos hoped to gain credibility with his Columbia Ph.D. In Sikkim as he learned written Tibetan he began translating a history of the life of Padma Shambava (called Guru Rinpoche in Tibetan).

When the idea of traveling to Gyantse took hold Theos began to learn spoken Tibetan which is very different from the written form—also there are two almost different spoken languages. Theos never became fluent in the formal language used by officials and nobles. He depended on a translator and describes his anxiety when meeting alone with politically important men, but then reports with elation that he managed to converse despite his inadequacies. There are four major dialects and many local variations of the language of the common people. Theos learned enough everyday Tibetan, as it was spoken in the Lhasa region, to deal with the Tibetans he hired to transport his belongings and to converse with people he met as he travelled.

Alexandra David-Neel became fluent in a dialect of the Amdo region of northeastern Tibet where she spent several years studying and translating texts. She was able to maintain her disguise as a pilgrim because her strange accent could be attributed to having come from a distant region.

Theos got permission to visit Gyantse with little difficulty because he had become friendly with many British officials, including David Mac-Donald who was the British Trade Agent for many years. His great stroke of luck was to arrive in Gyantse on the eve of the most auspicious day of the year—the day Buddha attained enlightenment. He impressed the abbot at Gyantse's monastery with his knowledge of both the language and Buddhism to such an extent the abbot suggested Theos might be an incarnation of a Guru Rinpoche. Theos did nothing to discourage this supposition. His unexpected welcome immediately fired his ambition to go on to Lhasa.

In Gangtok, Sikkim, Theos had met Rinchen Dolma's sister, whose husband was Tsarong Shappé. He was an influential member of the kashag, the lay government cabinet, had been educated in England, and was one of the wealthiest men in Tibet. Rinchen Dolma and her husband, Jigme Taring, the second son of the Raja of Sikkim, owned an estate about seven miles outside Gyantse. Rinchen Dolma and Jigme were approximately Theos' age and they invited him to dinner several times during the month of May while he was waiting for permission to go on to Lhasa. Rinchen Dolma wrote to her sister and asked that Tsarong initiate an invitation from the kashag to Theos. This and other string pulling by both clergy and lay officials, petition writing and gift sending, finally resulted in permission for a three-week stay in Lhasa.

In Lhasa Theos met the most important nobility and lamas. His stay was extended to an unprecedented three months. The Regent granted him several audiences and even wrote a letter, which he asked Theos to deliver to "the king of your country." Theos attempted to explain the status of Franklin Roosevelt and promised to deliver the letter. Theos translated the letter as follows:

> To His Excellency the great Mr. Roosevelt, President of America, White House, Washington,D.C.V.,E.C.I., the bearer of this letter, a citizen of your country, (kingdom), Mr. Theos Bernard, has great faith in the Buddhist Religion, and is possessed of great wisdom, mild and a good disciple. Especially has he the greatest desire to cement the friendship between Tibet and America. It is of importance that all of you who are concerned, should have a high regard for this matter, and render such assistance as lies in your power, in order that Buddha's doctrine may prosper exceedingly in all directions. This letter is sent by the Regent of Tibet, the Hu-thuk-thu of Ra-dreng Monastery, from the Happy Grove of the All-Good Beautiful Palace of the Thi-de Gan-Den Sam-Ten-Ling, on the Auspicious Date the tenth day of the eighth month of the Fire-Bull year. (September 1937)[21]

The letter was imprinted with a large square red seal of the Regent of Tibet. I have not been able to find a record that the letter was delivered to Roosevelt. I know that Theos' wife was extremely conscientious about responsibilities so I feel sure the letter was delivered, possibly via a New York Congressman.

During June, Theos met Seydam Cutting and his wife who had been allowed to return to Lhasa for a second visit, but for only two weeks. In letters to his wife he gloated about meeting many more officials and seeing many more closed institutions than the Cuttings. Likewise, he was very pleased that he had freedom of the city and monasteries while Tucci sent expensive gifts and endless entreaties which were not even answered.

Theos learned the mantras, prostrations, and offering rituals and was

66

invited to take part in ceremonies in all the monasteries he visited. He reports long talks about theology with abbots and especially learned teachers (*geshes*) although he didn't record exactly what they talked about in either his book or his diaries. According to his own account, he was initiated, on the eve of his departure from Lhasa, by the Tr'i Rimpoche, head of the Gelupka sect at Gandan Monastery. Theos does not say he took vows as a lama although later in the U.S. he let himself be publicized as "the white lama." Although he describes a three-day meditation ordeal in a sealed cell, like so many who write about mystical or transcendental experiences, he uses the word "indescribable" and stops there. He concludes his description of the ceremonies at Ganden:

> [The Tr'i Rimpoche] pointed out to me that now I had gained contact with an old soul that was within me; this was he said, the reason for my pilgrimage, that I had by no means come as a disciple to acquire learning, that I had, indeed, previously possessed this knowledge, and that it had been only a question of making the contact. Now, having brought consciousness into it, he said, it would be possible for me to continue my development throughout life.[22]

Theos returned to the United States with a collection of Tibetan scripture, other literature, and many artifacts. He bought, and was sometimes given, many rare and important items—so many he had to hire seventy pack animals to carry his belongings out of Tibet. He hoped to build a Tibetan-style monastery at which these books would be translated by lamas brought to the United States. However, he did not succeed in building a monastery; the books he collected are now at the Yale University library. Theos' story has been questioned, just as Alexandra David-Neel's exploits were.

"When one travels alone, it's your word against everyone else," Heinrich muttered, having eavesdropped on my explanation.

"Do you believe me?" Theos asked me.

Yes. I've seen how kind and warm the Tibetans can be. Besides I've seen part of your diary and your letters to your wife. However, I've found contradictions and some interesting omissions in your published materials.

Alexandra was beside Theos. "Well, we know what we did, don't we? And if others find it incredible, it's their failure, not ours. We must have some talks, Theos, I wish we could have met while we were alive."

You two talk while I explore Drepung.

Seventy or eighty percent of the monastery has been destroyed. Buildings were no longer whitewashed so it has ceased to look, even from the proper distance, like an auspicious pile of rice. We visited assembly halls and shrines, which tend to run together in my mind, but each monastery we visited had its own character and showed us a different aspect of monastic life in Tibet. (At least as it is today, which bears little resemblance to what it was like earlier in the century.)

My most lasting impression from Drepung was the students. Buddhism—the study of the mind—continues, although not by the thousands. Today the Chinese authorities decree how many may study at any monastery. BK said that, as in Theos' day, the monastery may hold more than the official number. In any case, only a tiny percentage of Drepung's buildings remain and an even tinier percent of lamas and novices live there. The few surviving elder lamas are not allowed to pass on the higher learning that previously sustained Tibetan Buddhism. The purest and more rigorous continuation of these traditions now must take place in diaspora where senior lamas still teach the traditional way.

"It's so silent." Theos was beside me. "A ghost town, absolutely eerie. You can't imagine how busy Drepung was. Lamas were everywhere. The Potala has become a museum but this is a supposed to be a functioning monastery."

As we wandered about we saw very few monks. One or two collected fees for photography, a few crossed courtyards on some errand, some relaxed in the kitchen. As we walked across a terrace outside one of the larger assembly halls with a view of Lhasa beyond, I looked toward the

Potala, where yesterday I had looked toward Drepung. I asked, Theos, is this the terrace of the photo in your book?

"I don't think so. It's all so strange, I can't really tell. Would you quote some of what I wrote about that morning? It was really an extraordinary experience."

> It was necessary to start at three in the morning for Drepung monastery in order to be there at sunrise, the time for the ceremonies in which I was expected to take part....At that point the heavens were still a misty mackerel, with the early morning colors visibly changing, and adding to the quiet ecstasy, which seemed to be in the very blood...
>
> It was the thrill of a lifetime to arrive at the top and find all the monks seated in long lines on the paved pavilion waiting to catch the first glimpse of the rising sun. The general effect of this seething mass of bareheaded men in reddish-brown homespun was that of a swarm of bees, for they were mumbling their precious mystic formula and counting off their beads, as with a furtive curiosity they observed the arrival of the bearded foreigner in Tibetan dress.
>
> ...with the break of day the trumpets, the horns, the conch shells and cymbals burst into sound and continued until the sun had drifted out of its shining crib. This was followed by the deep rumbling of the chants, which, I warrant, would send quivers up any one's spine. Within this great hall was another of their chief potentates, this time carrying his own emblem of authority, and after each chant it came down with a thud, which made the entire room vibrate with submission.[23]

Shussh-shussh, Theos I think I hear those bees you just mentioned.

We followed the sound and discovered a wonderful garden hidden in the heart of the monastery. A warm sun sifted through the small, dusty-green leaves of willow trees. The ground was covered with gray pebbles that must have come from a river bed for they are all softly rounded and look comfortable, in so far as stones can be comfortable. This protected courtyard in the heart of Drepung monastery, walled around by buildings, protected from winds, shaded from the sun and divided into areas by the old willows feels timeless.

Fifty or sixty fourth form students were debating in the courtyard. Pemba said they were nearly at the end of their courses after which, if they passed their examinations, they will be eligible to take their vows. The students who were between fifteen to eighteen years old sat in groups of five or six. In each group one stood expounding, delivering his view on a theological point, others sat listening. When a conclusion or an especially dramatic argument was made the orator slapped his hands together in a brushing motion as if to throw the idea into the laps of his listeners. Sometimes a listener responded, sometimes not.

As we entered the gateway, they looked up at us, some stared briefly, they were curious but they went on with their lessons throwing glances at us now and then. I took a few photographs then settled on a stone wall to watch, fascinated by these young men, all deeply involved in preparing themselves to carry on the future of their unique form of Buddhism.

Their robes are of various heavy fabrics in shades of red that range from dusty rose through cranberry to pigeon blood ruby. They wear skirts to their ankles and a sleeveless undershirt. Cumberbunds hold the skirts up and girdle the large shawl-like overgarment that they draped around their upper body, very often leaving one arm bare. Some of the debaters have hung their shawls on branches of nearby trees so they can gesture more dramatically as they talk.

They wear an enormous variety of shoes, from sandals to sneakers to all sorts of leather styles—definitely third world shoes. The sneakers are cheaply made and so unstylish by Western standards that no ghetto kid in the U.S. would want them in his house, let alone on his feet. The shoes and the often holey socks reflected their poverty.

"Excuse me..." Heinrich was beside me. "I'm sorry to interrupt your thoughts but you might explain that what these students are doing is a real mental workout. I was privileged to see the Dalai Lama himself take part in just this kind of debate here at Drepung."

It's amazing what you were able to see, Heinrich.

"Actually that came about almost accidentally. I had had breakfast with the Dalai Lama's brother Lobsang, who, as I think you know, was also a recognized incarnation. Since I arrived in Lobsang's company no one stopped me."

This very garden? I asked feeling a little thrill.

"You know, I think it might have been. With so much changed I've somewhat lost my bearings. But it might have been this courtyard. As I wrote:

> In front of a dark grove of trees a great multitude of red-cowled monks, perhaps two thousand of them, squatted on the gravel, while from a high place the Dalai Lama preached on Holy Writ....He spoke without any embarrassment and with the assurance of a grown man. This was his first public appearance. The fourteen-year-old boy had been studying for many years and now his knowledge was being tested before a critical audience.
>
> ...The Dalai Lama sat down on the gravel, so as not to emphasize the superiority of his birth, while the abbot in whose monastery the discussion was taking place stood before him and punctuated his questions with the conventional gestures. The Dalai Lama answered all the questions which were put to him, even the "teasers," with readiness and good humor and was never for a moment put out of countenance.

> After a while the antagonists changed places and it was the
> Dalai Lama who put questions to the seated abbot. One
> could see that this was not an act prepared to show off the
> intelligence of the young Buddha; it was a genuine contest
> of wits in which the abbot was hard put to it to hold his
> own.[24]

The courtyard with it's graceful trees and splattered light glowed like an Impressionist painting. The young men were magnificent in their vivacity. In this spot generations and generations of monks have repeated the dance-like gestures to the song of their own voices. The debating boys are learning the same texts in the old way, but the Tibet they were born into, the Tibet outside these walls, which allows curious Americans to invade this courtyard, is very different than sixty years ago when Theos Bernard was the first Western scholar to take part in ceremonies here.

I sat on the stone wall a long time, trying to guess where the animated students fit in. These young men grew up post-Cultural Revolution. They, and probably their parents, were born under Communism. Most of them have been here since they were six or seven years old. I don't know if they consider themselves lucky to be allowed to study in a monastery. Maybe they have a calling or maybe their parents chose this life for them. To what extent do the Chinese control their lives? Drepung seems to have quite a few students, but hardly any elders. How many actually live here, perhaps no one knows. Some of these lamas may be government spies; most anti-government protests are led by monks and nuns and many are now in Chinese jails, sometimes being tortured, as international human rights organizations continue to document.

The monasteries were formerly bastions of wealth; vast lands that once belonged to them are no longer theirs. How will these young men live? What will they do? Are they to be the teachers of the next generation of monks? Or are they doomed to years of boredom stationed in shrines, reminding tourists to pay the fee for indoor photography, wiping the floor free of dirt after the tourists have walked through, keeping the butter lamps alight, collecting the few bills placed by the devout and gathering at prescribed times to chant? Are they to be caretakers of museums rather than part of a living tradition?

When our group reconvened we wandered through the stony alley-ways. In a great, dark kitchen a wood burning stove was twice the size of my entire New York City kitchen. Huge copper ladles hung above the stove on which sat an enormous black iron pot. Bags of wheat and barley flour were stacked in a corner. Dozens of four foot tall churns stood against a wall. Heinrich returned to the monastery in 1982 and described the kitchens, "...No hot steam issuing from the kitchens, where monk-cooks, their faces soot-stained, used to stir their huge pots over clay-stoves fired with brushwood and yak dung."[25]

As we began to descend toward the parking area we heard a babble of voices more like crickets than the bee drone of the monks debating. Through a short passage we found another courtyard, this one without trees, simply surrounded by two-story cloistered buildings with faded, peeling paint. Here, little boys, five to seven years old, sat in groups of twenty or more memorizing scripture, repeating verses under the watchful eyes of a pair of more senior monks. The little boys wore the same kinds of robes and dubious footwear as their bigger brothers. They were far more distractible. When they saw us they turned, gawked, whispered to one another. When we raised our cameras they made "v" signs with their fingers, sometimes behind one another's head to make "horns." Another class on a cloister balcony grinned and made more "v" signs like miniature—and huggable—Churchills and Nixons.

Our group was enchanted by these little boys; their teachers relaxed for a while, chatting with Pemba, BK, Mark and Sharon. I felt lucky to be with a group that has no specific timetable; I had plenty of time to simply look, absorb, and ponder. This, of course, allowed my phantom guides to fill in a few of the many gaps in my knowledge. Alexandra was the one who joined me here.

"You know, monastic life now seems to be nothing at all like I experienced the years I studied at the Kumbum in Amdo."

I'm amazed, Alexandra, how open the reputedly insular and zenophobic Tibetans were during the early years of this century. They were kind to you—

"In the monasteries, yes. Certainly not everyone in the countryside was. But, of course uneducated peasants had many fears—of strangers, authorities, magicians and demons."

Nevertheless you and Theos and a few others, as well, were allowed to study in monasteries.

"As he takes such pains to point out, only Theos was allowed into the Lhasa monasteries. But, in fact, the lamas have always been warm toward sincere students. I don't think you can blame them for turning back the various Protestant missionaries whose only reason for wanting to reach Lhasa was to impose a different belief on people whose religion they didn't even attempt to understand. Actually, off and on, from the 15th century Catholic missionaries—most notably Cappuchins—were allowed to stay in Lhasa.

As we were leaving Drepung, BK pointed to a building set apart from the rest of the monastery. "That's where the Nechung Oracle used to live," he said. "He was the official state oracle who went into trances and answered questions affecting government policies."

"Psst, psst. Tell them what I said about the Oracle," Theos said.

I was going to do that later. But okay, your description of how that little monastery was built has a Pandora-ish theme that I like:

> ...one of the past Dalai Lamas captured an evil spirit which was causing considerable destruction. After placing the evil spirit in a box, he flung it into the river. One of the Lamas of Drepung, having heard of it, sent a young disciple to fetch it, with the admonition not to open the box. The temptation, however, was so great that at this spot, immediately below the monastery, he opened it, it vanished. On

returning with the tale to his master, the latter said that wherever that spirit was kept, there prosperity would always come. So Nechung built in an oasis of trees, will always be a cloister of happiness, and the chief oracle who lives here is in contact with that spirit which he consults in order to be able to apprise the government on whatever problems may arise.[26]

Theos, several things about that story aren't logical.

"Who says Tibetan logic is the same as yours? Huh?"

"Believe me, the Nechung Oracle defied my understanding," Heinrich said. "It was always a curious experience to meet the State Oracle in ordinary life. I could never get accustomed to sitting at the same table with him and hearing him noisily gulping his noodle soup. His face was that of a nice-looking young man, and bore no resemblance to the bloated, red-flecked, grimacing visage of the ecstatic medium."

And here's your description of his trance.

[During a trance] I watched him closely, never taking my eyes from his face—not the slightest movement of his features escaped me. He looked as if the life were fading out of him. Now he was perfectly motionless, his face a staring mask. Then suddenly, as if he had been struck by lightning, his body curved upward like a bow....the god was in possession. The medium began to tremble; his whole body shook and beads of sweat stood out on his forehead. Servants went to him and placed a huge, fantastic head-dress on his head. This was so heavy that it took two men to carry it. The slender body of the monk sank deeper into the cushions of the throne under the weight of his monstrous mitre....

The trembling became more violent. The medium's heavily laden head wavered from side to side, and his eyes started from their sockets. His face was swollen and covered with patches of hectic red. Hissing sounds pierced through his closed teeth. Suddenly he sprang up. Servants rushed to help him, but he slipped by them and to the moaning of the oboes began to rotate in a strange exotic dance. Save for the music, his groans and teeth-gnashings were the only sounds to be heard in the temple. Now he started beating his gleaming breastplate with a great thumb-ring, making a clatter which drowned the dull rolling of the drums. Then he gyrated on one foot, erect under the weight of the giant head-dress...The medium became calmer...a Cabinet Minister stepped before him and threw a scarf over his head. Then he began to ask questions....While the Minister stood humbly there trying to understand the answers, an old monk took them down with a flying pen.[27]

"As I said," Heinrich told me, "I suspected it was the secretary-monk who was the true oracle. For what was said was garbled and incoherent but what the secretary wrote would be the answers giving direction to the ministers."

Heinrich, you and Alexandra report astonishing things that occurred in Tibet which I love reading and knowing about. From among those students we saw today, do you think anyone could ever learn those mediumistic powers?

"I can't answer that." Heinrich replied. "But from what I saw in 1982 and what I'm seeing here with you, I think your question may be irrelevant. Such practices are things of the past. I can't imagine they will ever be relevant or credible again."

SERA

The afternoon we visited Sera was perfect Indian summer weather—except, of course, in Asia "Indian summer" would mean something very different. The brilliant sunlight accounts for my memories of Sera being full of warmth and serene beauty. Both Waddell and Harrer mention that Sera means "rose" or that the monastery was named after a wild rose hedge that used to be seen there. Sera is graced with a great deal of fairly recent, exuberantly pretty art work.

Waddell's book has four photographs taken at Sera. One shows a mass of "lamas and acolytes going to Lhasa" outside the gates. The structure behind them no longer exists although his photograph of the "chief temple" is not very different than a snapshot I took. Since I used Theos' description to introduce Drepung, I'll use Waddell's to introduce Sera.

> It had a population of nearly 6000 monks...[it] was quite a little town of well-built and neatly white-washed stone houses with regular streets and lanes....It is a monastic university, and consists of three colleges...one for the elementary teaching of the doctrines and ritual—this is the

Student monks debating with typical gestures

largest—another for friars who go about itinerating over the country, and the most select and smallest, the esoteric and mystical. All of these meet daily in the great Assembly Hall, which provides a joint temple for the whole community. It is a fine building.[28]

Alexandra has come along. "Monasteries were, indeed, basically towns. I think I'm uniquely qualified to give some information about that. It might be informative for you to give my description.

Quite right, Alexandra, and I'm also happy to note that for a woman, age has its privileges.

A large monastery in Tibet is a veritable town, the population of which sometimes amounts to as many as ten thousand persons. It is composed of a network of streets and alleys, squares and gardens. Temples in larger and smaller numbers and assembly halls of the different colleges, and the places of the dignitaries rise above the common dwellings, their gilded roofs and terraces surmounted by banners and divers ornaments. In the gompa every lama lives by himself in a house of which he is sole proprietor, whether he has had it built at his own cost or bought or inherited it. This dwelling may be bequeathed by the lama to one of his pupils or to a relative...No layman is allowed to possess a house in a monastery...

I had the privilege, unique in these days, of living in several monasteries. After what I have said of them, and of their separate houses, one can understand how it was possible for a woman to live there. Never the less, there is a rule against such admission, and only very special reasons—my age, the studies I was pursuing, and, above all, powerful protection—procured me this privilege.[29]

As at Drepung, the assembly halls of the colleges were inhabited only by cloaks and caps and a monk or two at the chapels. Here, too, in a less sheltered but also serene courtyard fifty or so young monks were debating. A few Tibetans, young mothers with silent children as well as older people, watched, apparently as fascinated as we were. As at the Potala and Drepung we saw less than a dozen other Westerners. Although I think tourists who don't go to monasteries miss the most representative part of Tibetan culture, I was glad to be with a small and unintrusive group.

Sera's most venerated chapel is to the "horse headed Buddha," a very old statue that supposedly has curative power. As always we circumambulated the shrine clockwise, feeling our way along the dark, narrow passage behind the statue. The walls were greasy from centuries of butter lamps. When I reached the statue, which had a blue horses's head with flaring nostrils, like those ahead of me, I knelt in the niche that allowed one to touch his forehead to the foot of the statue. A guardian monk firmly pushed my head against the statue and held it there for a moment. I had a flash of memory of being held under water by a minister when I was thirteen and baptized by total immersion at a quarry pond. When I stood the monk put a knotted kathag around my neck— a blessing. I wondered if I would feel more positive about Christianity today if the minister had given me a token, a cross or Bible, instead of letting me stand there like a wet cat, shivering and feeling a little silly and not at all changed by baptism.

All monasteries are full of pattern and design: hundreds or thousands of statues and murals showing aspects of Buddha, lives of famous lamas and teachers. Sera seems to have cornered the latest shipments of paint and to have attracted the most artists. Every corner we turned offered another vision of artistic exuberance. On the roof of the main assembly hall one of the buildings displayed enlarged versions of the *tsakali*, the eight auspicious symbols of the body, speech, mind, excellence, and activity of Chenresig. Recently painted and owing a debt of design to Chinese calendar art, they were a little faded from the sun but blended beautifully with peachy-brown plaster walls. On a nearby building were older paintings. Some had almost entirely faded away but one had an especially charming depiction of the harmony of the animals: where a long legged elephant stands with a monkey on his shoulders, and on the monkey's shoulder sits a hare, and on the hare's head stands a bird. The elephant is looking with wrinkled brow at a tree around which a serpent twines. Under a portico facing that wall are recent paintings of half a dozen Taras, red, white, green and black complexioned, each dancing, as they always do, inside a medallion. Tara, or Dolma, as she is known in Tibetan, is a female deity that is consort to Chenresig, the Buddha of Compassion.

Near the profusion of paintings we discovered the monastic version of the corporate corner office when we briefly visited the abbot of Sera in his private room. We passed through a small kitchen with a stove, a supply of wood, and a big kettle for making tea. The abbot, a middle aged man, tolerated our curiosity. His windowed corner room has a spectacular view of Lhasa valley. Only about twelve feet square, the room contained a built-in bed/settee covered with rugs—the typical sitting/sleeping arrangement of Tibetan homes. The room also held some small square tables with painted decorations and an altar with brass offering bowls, a small Buddha statue and a small picture of the Dalai Lama. Brilliant sunlight warmed the room and made it welcoming. In contrast, outside along the cloistered area, were several simple iron cots with thin blankets where other monks slept.

In the assembly hall of one of the smaller colleges, I exclaim to Ruth, "Look up!" Above the altar the ceiling was canopied with patchwork quilts! Ruth and I are quilters, and we immediately recognized patterns known in America as Nine Patch, Split Rail, Ocean Waves and Monkey Wrench. I gaped at the quilts a long time, trying to imagine how they had come to hang there. While quilted clothing has been used in China for hundreds of years and patchwork fabrics have been used in India a very long time, no early photographs from Tibet show any quilting at all. The patterns of those quilts were uniquely American and only in the last fifty years or so have spread widely around the world. Perhaps these quilts were less than fifty years old, although they looked very much like late 19th century quilts I've seen in these patterns. If they were newer the soot of the burning lamps could have discolored them the way 18th century green and yellow dyes in American quilts have turned brown. In the dim light I simply couldn't judge their age or the fabrics they were constructed of. Finally, I had to consider it one of the mysteries of Tibet.

A few of us went into a workroom where prayers were being block printed on strips of paper. The room was a mini-assembly line, at the end of which a monk with a couple of assistants folded the papers into little two-by-two-inch packages which the monk tied with knotted blue string. These were amulets that would be blessed and sold to pilgrims. The printers worked in pairs. One handled the paper, taking an individual sheet from a neat stack, laying it on the printing block and removing it when printed. Meanwhile his co-worker quickly inked the block with a brush and then, when the paper was in place, rapidly ran a roller over it. Both worked very fast, the inker with particular speed and precision. One pair of workers were father and four- or five-year-old son. The child handled the paper very accurately, and as he worked he sang in a clear childish voice.

"What's he singing?" I asked Pemba.

"Counting. One, two, three..."

"Tibetans always sing while they work," Theos said. "Remember? I wrote that they have a different song for every job."

But this is the first singing I've heard—except for the Chinese soldiers.

"Maybe it got killed off like the Jokhang's mice."

Rinchen Dolma is here too. "Oh, we used to sing about everything. The streets and courtyards and kitchens and workplaces were full of singing from morning to night. And such fun! Young people always thought of jingles and ditties, witty, satiric ones about whatever was going on in the city. Almost as soon as some clever person thought of a new song, someone else added another verse. But when the Chinese came, they caught on that the songs mocked them. People were arrested...and disappeared. The Chinese couldn't tell the difference between an innocent folk song and a political one so they passed a law that no one was allowed to sing in the streets. Even at home singing wasn't safe."

"When I think of Tibet, I think of music," Theos said. "Even traveling on mountain trails, the bells on the yaks and donkeys were a merry sound on the lonely roads. They were also a warning on narrow paths that they were approaching."

As we climbed above the monastery we passed several rock paintings which were recently touched up with brilliant blues, yellows and reds. Many showed the blue protective deities wearing necklaces of human skulls. Near inspection revealed the paintings were especially lively because they were very low bas reliefs.

On the hillside above the monastery was a grid of pipes covering an area of about seventy by fifty feet. Pemba explained, "This is a place to display the great thanka. It's shown only once a year."

Theos grabbed my arm. "Oh! Is that what that is? How modern of them! I'll tell you all about—"

Shussh-shussh, Theos, not now. I know you have your story to tell. Save it until we get to Gyantse.

"Theos," Alexandra said, taking his arm, "come tell me about the ceremonies here. I would have loved to have seen all you did."

"Well, Madam Neel—"

"*David*-Neel, please try to remember!"

"Sorry, I'm not used to hyphenated names. The monasteries are a man's world."

"I know, but I was a scholar too. We're colleagues. Let's go up there where the rock paintings are. We'll have a bird's eye view."

I sat at the foot of the thanka structure as the others climbed about and took pictures. Sitting in the sun, shedding layers of clothing, I was lost in the silence—a kind of silence that can't be found in any western populated area of this size. Not a motor was heard, no cars, trucks, airplanes, no mechanical equipment, no sirens, no jackhammers, no honks or beeping back-up signals, no telephones, radios, TVs, boom-boxes, no clicking computer keyboards or door bells.

Each major monastery has—or used to have—a great thanka, hundreds of square feet in size which is kept rolled up throughout the year but on the day in early summer when Buddha's enlightenment is celebrated, it is taken to a specially constructed display area and unrolled. A platoon of monks are needed to carry and unroll it. It may be displayed for other important days, but always very briefly.

In Kathmandu, BK had arranged a lecture about thankas. The eight of us barely fit in the tiny shop of a thanka dealer who insisted we all sit on stools, several of which had to be borrowed from neighboring shops. The English speaking proprietor used his collection of thankas as illustration as he explained their uses and iconography.

Thankas are paintings on fabric, sometimes silk but mostly sturdy canvas. Inexpensive mass printed thanka posters are for sale in Kathmandu or Lhasa. The dealer's thankas had been hand-painted for home altars; they were unframed. In monastery assembly halls, thankas hang from the ceiling, each framed in brilliantly colored brocade. Old thankas (any over fifty years is usually considered old) are often tan from the smoke of butter lamps and incense and are permeated with the scent of that smoke.

A large variety of religious subjects may be painted on thankas, but the majority show the various forms of Buddha. I was enchanted to learn that the blue deities' hair standing on end symbolizes enlightenment—a feature also of the snow lions' manes. The thanka dealer patiently explained the aspects of Buddha, the meaning of the various animals pictured, and that some of the pictures were actually maps of the Buddhist metaphysical world, much like mandalas.

My attention wandered, as it's apt to do when I'm among people speaking a language I don't understand. Tibetan art is so complex and so different from Western art that my education and appreciation will take several more years.

As I sat near the thanka structure at Sera, an old woman walked past covering her face so no one would photograph her, a couple of men wandered by, a goat nibbled his way across the hillside. We had a long view down at the stair-stepped rooftops of the monastery with their shining bronze ornaments. Beyond, Lhasa Valley spread to the distant mountains. I do not know what proportion of its former size Sera Monastery now is. Many buildings were leveled here but the evidence of destruction has been removed. It's hard to imagine that not only a million human beings but thousands of native stone buildings can be among the "disappeared" like the Argentinian political activists.

BK mentioned a book about "power places" in Tibet. This new age idea did not appeal to me but I do feel that ancient places, ruined or intact, stir our imagination as we wonder about generations that have walked or sat on the same stones. I sat in the Egyptian sun like this at Hatshepsut's temple to Hathor and I sat in the Greek sun at Delphi near what once was the temple to the pythoness. At Masada I leaned against a wall watching heat mirages over the Dead Sea. I can't imagine myself living the lives of people from such different cultures and times. But I believe that people have chosen to build in places that give them a sense of safety and well being—which often has meant wide vistas. So the sense of peace and contentment I enjoyed at Sera is inspired by the view of the valley, the blue sky that promises no storms today and the gentle warmth of the sun on my face and hands. Generations of Tibetans have shared those feelings here on this mountain side.

Woman vender of jewelry and trinkets

BARKOR

One morning in Lhasa I circumambulated the Jokhang with Elizabeth and Denise. We had come to worship that god of the female traveler, Souvenir Shopping. Our "holy" quest was for treasures—necklaces, earrings, bracelets, rings, and small packable items for family and friends from one of the fabled bazaars of Central Asia. I felt like humming Borodin's music. The sky was clear, the air was crisp and I was among a wonderful assortment of people and things.

The Barkor, as the street circling the Jokhang is called, is lined with market stalls and tables, as are the small streets radiating from it. The ground floor of the houses along the Barkor serve as shops. Tables of inexpensive jewelry mingle with useful items: small rugs, Chinese lidded teacups, skeins of wool, bolts of the striped fabric for women's aprons, shawls, wonderfully embroidered felt boots, tea kettles, daggers, cheap polyester brocades for blouses, scratchy worsteds for men's jackets, knitted sweaters mostly in cheap acrylics that scream "Made in China", sheaves of printed prayers, inexpensive sun hats, baby clothes, statues of deities and snow lions, antelope and wild sheep's horns, amulet boxes, and much more—a marvelous miscellany.

BK had said that, as always in the past, when country people come to Lhasa on pilgrimage they bring a treasure or two which they sell to venders to pay for their trip, or at least part of their expenses. "If you look very carefully," he said, "you might find a true antique, but they're rare. Almost anything of real worth was sold long ago." He explained further, "Most jewelry is actually made in Nepal. Many of the stones, especially turquoise, coral and amber are fake."

The Barkor was a great place to people watch. True pilgrims, usually dressed in country clothes, prostrated at every step. Some threw their body forward again and again. Others progressed crabwise, measuring their prostrations by their body width. People walked past the pilgrims, paying as little attention to them as the pilgrims paid to the rest of the crowd.

I loved seeing the Khampas—people from Kham, an eastern province of Tibet. They were often taller than other Tibetans, their jet black hair was always adorned, the men's with hanks of red yarn tied above an ear with the fringe hanging down, and the women's with beads of turquoise and amber. Men and women both wore beaded earrings. The women chose brightly colored blouses and many necklaces, bracelets, rings. The men's robes were homespun in a rich shade of brown that may have come from vegetable dyes. Their posture was proud and they turned away with natural dignity when I attempted to photograph them, almost as if by instinct, neither cringing or challenging, simply avoiding what was apparently distasteful to them. The Khampas were the most beautiful people I had ever seen.

Waddell had positioned himself squarely in the middle of the passageway, standing soldier-straight, looking up and down.

They're worth watching, aren't they, Colonel?

"Oh, yes, they're magnificent looking people."

Heinrich emerged from a dark shop that sold men's fedoras and joined us. He was shaking his head and chuckling. "They're still wearing those ridiculous hats that make them look like a lot of Chicago gangsters," he said. "They were doing that in the '40s; I thought they'd have given them up by now."

In the Andes the Inca women still wear English bowler hats. What I admire is the dress and demeanor of the Khampas.

"It's funny," Heinrich said, again shaking his head, "When I first came to Tibet 'Khampa' was synonymous with brigand. They were the last people you wanted to meet if you were traveling alone through the Eastern mountains. Travelers and nomads were terrified of them."

But that's not true any more.

"No. Though I see no one has been able to get them to give up their weapons. See, the men all have daggers at their waists." I looked. He was absolutely right. "They were wonderful fighters against the Chinese. Did you know your CIA flew some to the Rocky Mountains and trained them in guerrilla warfare?"

Yes, I knew that. But the CIA's involvement was too little too late.

"I have no idea what you're talking about," Waddell said. "But it's nice that they're here because they are about the only exotic element these days. The Barkor was much more colorful and exciting in 1904. I found it quite fascinating then. I think it's rather appalling now. Hardly more exotic than Petticoat Lane on a Sunday morning."

I was hoping what you wrote would still be true, Col. Waddell.

"But we're here to show just the opposite, that nothing is the same. I believe that's the essence of our function," Waddell reminded me.

I love it when you surprise me, Colonel. I was very taken by your description.

> The bazaar was always attractive with its human kaleidoscope of changing form and color....you could see nearly everyday coming in from the North, a caravan of travel-stained nomads from Mongolia and the Russian steppes of Siberia. The ruddy-cheeked stalwart men in dingy yellow woolen and felt suits or greasy sheepskins ride unkempt

ponies and [were] armed with spears and matchlocks...their fair complexioned women, also mounted, are covered with bright silver and brass trinkets stuck all over their dresses and tied into the long plaits of their hair, help their spouses to escort their valuables laden on double-humped Bactrian dromedaries....

In the cosmopolitan crowd, you see shiny-pated ruby-robed monks moving about amongst the drab and purple-clad populace, or mingling picturesquely with the blue and yellow-coated richer classes and bejeweled townswomen in all their silks and finery. You see indigo-gowned pallid Chinese in their self-complacent pride, the half-bred "Kokos," white-turbanned Mohamedan merchants and Turks from Ladak, Kashmir and Tartary...and the quaintly garbed country-folk from the distant provinces—the upstanding athletic Khams from the east with the fine physique and free carriage of mountaineers, wearing a thick fringe of hair over their brows, the diversely-clad men and women from Tsang and the west and the squat begrimed people of the Lower Tsangpo, many of whom are utter barbarians of a very low type and entirely in the skins of wild beasts.[30]

I'd love to see some dromedaries.

Theos had joined us. He said, "Domedaries are a startling sight at such an altitude even though the climate is very desert-like.

"So you saw them too?" Waddell asked.

"The ones I saw weren't here at the Barkor," Theos answered. "I was riding around Chakpori toward Norbulinka one day and reached a spot where it was possible to look down upon animals grazing. Much to my surprise, I saw a large herd of light-colored Mongolian camels. Of all the places where I had expected to find camels, Lhasa was about the last. But then I remembered that these camels had been used to cross the great Chang-Tang plain. These animals had belonged to the late Dalai Lama, and were now having an opportunity to rest."[31]

Nowadays, the people visiting the Barkor come from fewer places and they dress more alike. Despite highways and an airport, Lhasa is less a crossroad now than it was early in the century. The whole world is becoming homogenized with sneakers and tee-shirts everywhere.

"Well," observed Waddell, "Tibet certainly was never an isolated country, though they protected their holy city from Westerners—commerce is always what counts, you know."

"Why, Colonel—" said Alexandra, who had acquired a hand held prayer wheel that she turned as she talked, "I do believe you enjoyed being here."

"Madam Neel, did you think I didn't?"

"*David*-Neel. I certainly thought you didn't. You were so unkind about the Tibetans."

"You do me an injustice, Madam. If a little more of my passage about the bazaar could be quoted, you'd see. Will you quote more, please? I'm not an ogre. I think of myself as quite a sensitive man."

Most men do.

"Don't mumble like that," Waddell snapped at me. "If you're going to complain speak up—so I can refute you."

It was a feminist reflex. I'll be sure to speak up loud and clear in the future. Here's your quote.

> ...Their beardless faces, though coarse-featured and small and restless-eyed, had a contented cheery expression....Their friendly demeanour did not bear out Marco Polo's wholesale denunciation, that "The people of Tebet are an ill-conditioned race." It was almost always a good-humored grinning crowd that gathered round us in our shopping and photographic excursions and smiled in childish pleasure at our lavishness, or stared with open-eyed curiosity at our strange ways, invariable respectful though never cringing.[32]

"You caught them well, Colonel," Alexandra said. "We Europeans thought they were childlike because we've lost the capacity for wonder, I think."

"I agree entirely," Theos spoke up.

"I can see, Theos," Alexandra said, "you must have caused waves of head turning here in the Barkor, walking around in your Tibetan robes with that unkempt reddish-brown beard."

"The Tibetans were endlessly curious, not only about my appearance, but about all my habits and my possessions. Their eagerness to see and touch everything was alternately charming and maddening."

Yes, your typewriter story is a perfect example.

"I'm glad you saw part of my diary. I couldn't include everything in my book. My editor wasn't as generous with space and pages as Col. Waddell's editor was."

I'm glad you took a portable Smith Corona on your trip to keep a diary and write letters because your handwriting is really difficult.

Theos grinned at me, "That may be the pot calling the kettle black."

> The first thing after my arrival was to write up the notes of the day which meant that everyone about the place had to come in to have a look...[at] the strange individual they were housing upstairs and what he was doing....It takes them so long to write out a couple words that they look upon this [machine] with the greatest amazement. When I am not using it they want to caress it like a child and delicately press all the keys. I have placed a sheet of paper in it at times for one of the Shappés and others of higher ranks and they have sat down and run off the alphabet as it is organized on the keyboard without making any change, and then those who know the English letters, will patiently pick out their name and be as proud of the results as a kindergarten child. It is truly most touching to watch them in their unsophisticated action, but I also must say that I

could commit murder every now and then, for the machine draws them like a freshly sown field brings the sparrows which all means that I have no privacy...not being satisfied to stand at the door, they will first walk in and drape themselves around the pole in the middle of the room and then when they feel that their presence has become familiar, they will commence the attack...they have to put their nose down into the letter chamber and watch each letter as it is printed.[33]

"You hit the privacy matter squarely on the head, the very concept of privacy did not exist," Alexandra said. "Imagine having to maintain a disguise when staying with country people who invade even the personal activities that are most private for us in the West."

"Honesty makes life considerably easier, Madam," Waddell pointed out primly.

"You're here at a place you loved but you're still in a very disagreeable mood today," Alexandra said tartly.

Before Alexandra and the Colonel get into a fight, I ask Heinrich, "Was the Lhasa you remember from the '40s and '50s very different from what the Colonel described?"

"Well, it was not so exotic, but it was still a real marketplace for serious trading and commerce." Heinrich is a man of relatively few words. He gestured. "I'm happy to see people looking cheerier than they were in '82 when I came back. I was so depressed by the enforced drabness I almost wished I hadn't come. I see a lot of Chinese policemen or soldiers; I find that disturbing." For a moment we were all silent as we watched a pair of brown uniformed policemen walk though the crowded street—counterclockwise.

"But look," Theos said, "that house is freshly painted. That's a very positive sign." I looked at the three-story house with flowers stenciled in bright colors around the windows, geraniums in the window boxes, and new valances over them.

"Yes," Heinrich agree, "houses weren't all so prosperous looking, of course, but there was a sense of gaiety in Lhasa. In spite of the destruction and lack of freedom, the spirit of the people is strong."

"We should let her get on with her shopping," Alexandra said.

Any suggestions?

"Just walk around, don't be shy." Heinrich answered. "People love to bargain. If you don't bargain you'll spoil their fun and miss the give and take. And they need the money. When you buy trinkets, even stuff brought in from Nepal, you're giving them money, you're making their lives a little easier and getting a souvenir in return. Don't worry too much about the authenticity. It's the people who are authentic."

"Looky-looky," calls the woman behind the table of jewelry. She has a little calculator in her hand. We can bargain without knowing one another's language simply by punching the numbers. But she has enough English to say, "very old Tibeti silver. Very good, you buy."

I did.

After a morning amid the bustle of the Barkor, in the afternoon, I walked to the Kyichu River which was less than a mile south of the Holiday Inn. It marks the southern border of Lhasa, and is met by mountains on the other bank. I had walked down the broad street leading into the city from the airport road. It was lined with single story buildings— a strip mall, Lhasa style, containing Chinese businesses, small grocery stores, bicycle repair shops, hardware shops, a few restaurants, even a disco. I had passed the entrance to Norbulinka.

I loitered by the river that afternoon. Along this stretch of the river, west of the city, there is a long walk where a sward with aspens separates the river from a highway sparsely traveled by tractors and trucks. A couple of boys on bikes came up to me to practice their English asking, "Where are you from? What's your name? What time is it?" A matched pair of school girls strolled along the river bank with their bags of books. The pretty, slender girls settled shoulder to shoulder on the bank, talking to one another in that quiet, intense way of adolescent girls who are best friends and have many secrets to share—about teachers, brothers and sisters, parents, other girls in their class and most of all about boys.

I felt sure they were Chinese girls whose parents worked here in Lhasa. Perhaps they had been born here. In many ways they were like school girls everywhere but they were also Chinese in Tibet. Maybe their parents didn't even want to be here. Did the girls enjoy living in Lhasa? Did they have better educations and better opportunities for the future than Tibetan girls the same age? Did the teenage Tibetan boys find these girls glamorous compared to Tibetan girls? Did romances between Chinese and Tibetans start Romeo and Juliet-type feuds?

Those girls had something in common with the daughters of pioneers who settled the American West. Americans felt crowded in the cities and densely settled states along the Atlantic seaboard. The American continent was wide and rich and, in their eyes, empty. They settled the territories and worked hard building homes, clearing farm land and making the prairie bloom, as they were proud to say. They wanted a better life. Is Tibet the same to the Chinese? While not a rich farmland, Tibet is vast and fairly empty, a place with gold and other valuable minerals. Meanwhile the Chinese are destroying indigenous traditions as surely, and deliberately, as Americans nearly destroyed Native Americans and their culture.

As I strolled beside the river. I met elderly Tibetans, walking along with their rosaries and prayer wheels. Perhaps they were country people, pilgrims who had come to pray at the holy places in Lhasa. Some looked up at me and said softly, "Dalai Lama?" BK had warned against bringing pictures of the Dalai Lama although people would ask for them. Perhaps he was overly emphatic I thought when I saw that no one was around to see if I gave these people pictures. But I had none.

The riverside path ran atop a modern, well engineered levee that kept the Kyichu from flooding Lhasa. At rare places there were steps down to the river, but there was absolutely no traffic on the river nor any fishermen along its banks. I found Rinchen Dolma and Heinrich sitting beside the path, waiting for me.

"This is quite a fine piece of work," Heinrich said. "It goes well beyond the dam Aufschnaiter and I built in 1948. And we had quite a labor force because we expected the monsoons and snow melt higher up would soon send the river into Norbulinka's grounds." He had that slightly distant look of a man remembering a job well done long ago, a tone of quiet pride in his voice. "I was given a force of five hundred soldiers and a thousand coolies. No contractor in Tibet had ever had so many hands."

Not even when the Potala was built?

"Well, I don't know. I suppose if you go back that far—" A cloud of consternation crossed his face.

I was sorry I felt the need to cut his good memories down a bit, but we Westerners are reflexively short sighted about history.

"Heinrich, you are a good man and were a good builder," Rinchen Dolma said kindly. "You insisted you would not use forced labor and that the men were paid every day. This wall we're standing on was not built that way. The Chinese forced our people—men, women, and even children—to build it although many were sick, all were half-starved. Many people died. My sister was forced to carry stones on her back under the eyes of gun carrying guards." Her voice caught, she turned away from the levee.

Heinrich took a large, white handkerchief from his pocket and handed it to her.

"I'm sorry I'm so emotional..."

We look at a lot of fine examples of engineering like this levee and never think of the people who did the actual building.

"That's true," Heinrich said. "Like the Egyptian pyramids—slave labor."

And the pyramids in Mexico, the monuments left by Greece and Rome, roads, aquaducts, temples, ampitheatres.

"Yes, somebody had to do the backbreaking work," Heinrich agreed. "History books don't mention them."

"If there were more good men like Heinrich, the world would be a better place," Rinchen Dolma said. She took his hand as he blushed like a school boy.

"When I think of what the Chinese have done here, I get furious," Heinrich said. "I hate being on this side of the city even if it does look more modern than the crowded Tibetan part. I hate being surrounded by Chinese and their oblivious school children."

"We mustn't hate them," Rinchen Dolma said. "His Holiness the Dalai Lama says so. We will not recognize their claim to our country but we must love the people who are simply human as we are."

"I don't think I could ever be a good enough Buddhist to feel that way," said Heinrich.

Christians are supposed to love their enemies too.

"But we don't, do we?" Heinrich's voice rose. "It's not human nature."

"Buddhism teaches us to use the best part of our human nature and overcome the destructive parts," Rinchen Dolma said.

"Easy enough to say. Difficult to feel," Heinrich muttered, clenching his teeth.

I had reached the road that lead away from the river toward the Potala. I walked past the crowded park and the ostentatious plaza in front of the palace and went to the quiet park in back where I paid two yuan (twenty-four cents) and was given a ticket. The park had a scruffy, down-at-the-heels look. Nothing was cared for, although it was not littered. Grass grew sparsely, packed dirt paths meandered. Trees looked old, derelict. Probably because this park cost money it was not as crowded as the one in the front, but some groups were scattered about. Picnickers put up what looked like play pens made of fabric attached to five foot high posts. A sizable lake was surrounded by a low wall, overlooked by big, age-gnarled willows. Huge gold-colored fish swam by near the surface or leapt up with a splash, probably needing a little more oxygen than was available near the bottom where, I imagined, tons of leaves were rotting and turning the water the color of rootbeer.

I sat on a stone wall by the lake aware that I felt content to be alone in the middle of Lhasa. At this point in my life, I travel as a singleton, although I cherish solitude and privacy, being with a small group is very satisfying. Choosing to be part of a small group that gives ample free time suits my temperament, especially since my companions were thoughtful and interesting people. I often read tales of travelers of the past exploring foreign countries, most were alone only in the sense of having no companions from their own country. Nearly all hired local people as guides and porters.

"I quite understand being alone in a crowd," Waddell said. He stood nearby with a foot up on the wall, watching for fish. "A thinker has to have time to make notes and collect impressions. However, Tibet is not a country one travels to alone—or certainly couldn't in my time." A splash. "That one was at least a foot long, could have been three or four pounds!"

"I couldn't have made my trip alone," Alexandra said forcefully as she sat down beside me. She had arrived holding Lama Yongden by the arm. "Fortunately I had Apthur—the best possible companion."

I'm happy we can meet, Lama Yongden. Elizabeth gave me your novel, *Mipam*, which is still in print. I enjoyed reading it.

"Thank you very much, Madame. I'm glad to hear my book's still in print." Lama Yongden said with a toothy, boyish grin. "I was lucky to travel with Madame. We pretended to be a traveling lama and his old mother. Sometimes I said father was a *senygur* —a magician—and my mother had learned some of his magic." He chuckled.

"The country people were very superstitious, they gave a few coins or a handful of tsampa, a knob of butter to make sure we don't make magic against them," Alexandra said. "Some were miserly, some were generous—like people everywhere, good and bad. Traveling with a lama was a great help."

I know, too, that your pretense to be mother and son became reality.

"Yes, I legally adopted Apthur when we got to France," Alexandra said, giving Lama Yongden a fond smile. "I could never have borne and raised a better son. If all mothers could test the mettle of their sons on a trek on foot across Tibet before claiming relationship, imagine how fine the men of the world would be." She laughed.

"Companions are important," Heinrich agreed as he joined us. "Peter, please come here and meet the author just this one time." Aufschnaiter, serious and reserved, approached, smiling tentatively. Heinrich continued, "Without companionship I believe I might have given up during the long winter we wandered among the nomads. Peter's determination and perseverance kept me going when I was so cold and exhausted I wanted to give up."

I'm glad to meet you, Peter. I've seen you as a shadow at the edge of Heinrich's books.

"We were equally desperate," Peter said. "Being prisoners of war was bearable. But we certainly weren't properly fitted out for our ordeal, no gloves or mittens, entirely inadequate footwear."

"That's true, it's a miracle we have all our fingers and toes," Heinrich chuckled.

I turned to Theos. You didn't travel alone either.

"No, my translator, Tharchin, was a very fine companion. A scholar, a school teacher, a Tibetan who knew intellectuals throughout Tibet. We spent a lot of time with our heads together planning the best way to plead my case for being allowed to visit Lhasa. He was a godsend, good natured, trustworthy, and intelligent. Plus there were the boys who were with me when Tharchin went ahead to Lhasa."

That's an unfortunate term, Theos. Nowadays we try to be politically correct.

"What term?"

We no longer call servants of any nationality or race "boys."

"But everyone—" Theos began.

Everyone used to wear their bigotry like their suntans, as if their sense of superiority were earned because they had the money to be indolent. But now we know suntans lead to skin cancer and bigotry to social cancer.

Waddell cleared his throat. "Must you preach to us? We lived in our times, and you live in yours."

"Excuse me," Rinchen Dolma appeared. "I'd like to talk about travelling too."

"You travelled over the mountains a number of times, didn't you?"

"Yes, indeed. When I was a girl, and of course, when I was married, we traveled with many servants. But when the dreadful time came when the Dalai Lama had to flee, my husband who, was in charge of his guard, accompanied him. I remained in Lhasa briefly, deeply torn between following him and remaining with my elderly mother and our children and grandchildren. My family convinced me to go and I traveled with only one servant, Tashi, and one mule. Tashi was a wonderful man. He led me over the mountains I could never have crossed alone. He broke a path through the deep snow with his body, throwing himself full length again and again. He cooked for me and kept watch..." Her voice drops and tears come to her eyes. "And when I was safe in Kalimpong, Tashi left me to return to Tibet and share the fate of his family. I never heard what happened to him. In fact, for years, Jigme and I had no news of our family. When we finally learned our children had withstood severe hardship but were still alive we felt incredibly blessed. Excuse me ..." Rinchen Dolma walked away in tears.

As Rinchen Dolma walked away, I recalled the part of her book that I found most poignant. She explained that after she rejoin her husband and took up residence in Dharmsala with other refugees in 1959, they had no news about their children until 1979. Another ten years passed before the children—who were adults, of course—were allowed to visit Dharmsala.

Near the end of her book, Rinchen Dolma, who as a noble child had no idea of want or hunger, wrote:

> I try constantly to avoid the sorrow of selfishness, but my love and longing for my own children is always there, as any mother's would be. I miss them when I get good food to eat, I miss them when I am given plenty to wear—and especially when I see the pale moon I miss them, for we all can see the moon, yet we cannot meet.[34]

DRAK YERPA

"My favorite day," Felicity declared.

"Mine too," Elizabeth said.

"Perfect!" I called from the bathroom as I put moisturizer on my red nose—even 25SPF sun block hadn't prevented a little sunburn.

"If you told me a magician gave us those blue skies and that breeze, I'd believe you," Felicity said. She yawned and was asleep immediately.

I got into bed, thoroughly tired and thoroughly happy after a day hiking at Drak Yerpa. "We couldn't have had a better day if BK had had a weather oracle arrange it," I said.

Heinrich didn't see Felicity and Elizabeth, and, of course, they didn't see him either, but he was sitting on the foot of my bed, smiling in an avuncular way. "That was hardly mountain climbing, but maybe you can see why I love hiking in places like that."

Indeed I do.

"I told you about the weather oracle, didn't I?"

Yes, and so did Theos.

"Oh, Theos, Theos, you're lost little golden boy. The great authority. What did he learn in ten weeks? I lived here for seven years."

Meditation cave and chapel built into hillside

Yes, you did. The rainmaker's trance seems similar to the oracle's. "Perhaps, but the effects were more immediate."

After the Dalai Lama moved to his summer residence the weather became very warm, but not unpleasantly so...the air is dry and rain falls seldom. Soon everyone is praying for rain....the Oracle of Gadong, the most famous rainmaker in Tibet, is summoned to the garden of the Dalai Lama....The rainmaker, a monk, soon falls into a trance. His limbs begin to move convulsively and he gives utterance to strange groans. At that moment one of the monastic officials solemnly begs the oracle to vouchsafe rain and thereby save the harvest. The movements of the rainmaker become more and more ecstatic, and high-pitched words escape him. A clerk takes down the message and hands it to the Cabinet Ministers. Meanwhile the body of the entranced medium, now no longer possessed by the divinity, sinks unconscious to the ground and is carried out.

After the performance everyone in Lhasa excitedly waits for the rain. And rain it does....[The Tibetan] explanation naturally did not satisfy me and I tried to find a more scientific solution. The British Legation had set up a meteorological station and measured the rainfall scientifically. It amounted to an average of about fourteen inches a year and mostly occurred at this season. Aufschnaiter later installed a water-gauge on the Kyichu and recorded the first rise in the river level on almost the same day every year. Had he followed the rainmaker's methods he could have set himself up as a successful oracle. [35]

"So you see," Heinrich said, "your guide didn't need a weather oracle. It rains very little this time of year. Early autumn is an ideal time to be in Tibet."

I couldn't agree more. I'd love to do more hiking, and I'm sorry it's not in the plan. I fell asleep remembering a beautiful day.

At 9:00 that morning, we drove east on the well paved road that goes to China along the south side of the Kiychu river. We passed farm villages, one with the most beautiful black piglets I'd ever seen. The aspen and willow trees along the river flickered gold as the leaves moved in a light breeze. Wheat and barley fields were amber with ripe grain. The river sparkled, moving slowly. After about thirty miles we crossed a one-lane iron bridge. I wondered if it were one of the six iron bridges Theos said were built by Tsarong, his host who had been trained in England as a mechanical engineer. We doubled back westward on the other side of the river for two or three miles before turning up into the mountains toward Drak Yerpa. The road followed a stream and became more and more difficult, but our driver negotiated the ruts, and potholes, forded the stream several times. He missed boulders, met hay wagons, and crossed very narrow wooden bridges.

Far above us—looking deceptively near in the crystalline light, yet distant when I contemplated the uphill hike—were the little structures fronting chapels and meditation caves. Part way up sat a few farmers' houses, the ruins of a village and of a sizable monastery. Farther up, above the structures, were the dark mouths of caves in the cliff face. "Yerpa is a very holy site, one of Tibet's power places," BK told us. "I've come all six times I've been in Tibet and never seen other Westerners or Chinese—and I hope we don't today."

We stopped and picked up three monks, a middle-aged man and two boys, trudging along the road. Rinchen Dolma slipped in beside me. She whispered, "We used to come here in the summer. Will you quote my story of why Yerpa is a pilgrimage site, please?"

Yes, Rinchen Dolma, you know I always prefer your version of local history.

Buddhism suffered during the reign of King Langdarma (A.D. 803)...many pro-*Bon* people became government ministers. [*Bon* was the animistic religion that Buddhism had replaced but which continued in parts of Tibet.] They made new laws to destroy Buddhism, sealed up the principal temples and broke all the images....Langdarma made the Buddhist monks choose whether to marry, to carry arms or to become huntsmen. Death was the punishment for remaining Buddhist. But Langdarma was able to wipe out Buddhism only in Central Tibet and not in the more remote parts of the country.

Eventually things became so bad that a hermit—Lhalung Paldor—who was meditating in a cave at Yerpa, near Lhasa, decided to do something. He set out for Lhasa, wearing a black hat and black cloak, with charcoal and grease smeared on all his clothes and on his white horse, and his bow and arrow hidden in the long sleeves of his cloak. Outside Lhasa he tied his horse near the river, walked into the city and found Langdarma and some of his ministers in front of the Jokhang. Prostrating himself before Langdarma, Lhalung Paldor loosed an arrow from his bow straight at the King's heart and killed him. In the confusion that followed, Lhalung Paldor escaped to the river, mounted his horse and forced it to swim to the other bank to wash the charcoal away. Then, turning his cloak, and with his horse white again, he galloped to Yerpa and hid in his cave.... Although search parties were sent out in different directions no one could find a man on a black horse wearing a black coat and hat....A rumor that Lhalung Paldor had killed the King soon spread, so the hermit left his cave and took refuge in Eastern Tibet. His image was to be seen in many monasteries and there was also one in his cave at Yerpa. After Langdarma's death the nobility became supporters of Buddhism and founded many monasteries which lasted until the Chinese destroyed them recently.[36]

"Take your time, we'll be here all day. Rest when you feel like it," BK instructed, always practical. "Drink plenty of water, put on extra sun screen."

"*Kale-kale*," Elizabeth said. Her phrase book said it meant slowly, slowly. Theos walked beside me making an obvious effort to slow his young man's pace to my much slower one. He was very upset. "The more I see the more I understand how Heinrich felt in '82 when he returned. There was a wonderful monastery up there. And now nothing but ruins!"

You barely mentioned Yerpa in *Penthouse of the Gods*, but I came across your description in a letter. You called it the "high spot" of your trip east of Lhasa on your way to visit Ganden. Here's your description.

> Yerpa...enshrines the cave where Guru Rinpoche was wont to meditate, the place where Atisha used to stay, as well as the first images of the Tsug-lag-kang, the first temple of Tibet. To add more to this holy spot, the Lama who killed the King who was trying to uproot the beginnings of Buddhism during his short reign of three years came to this place and remained for some time after his escape....As a result of so many of Tibet's saints having used this holy spot tucked away in the heavens beneath overhanging cliffs of sandstone, it embodies a little of all the sects...
>
> I immediately commenced to find out if there were any hermits staying in the nearby caves, and as my good fortune would have it, there was, and I was given permission to visit him. He has been living in this cave now for ten years, having spent twelve years in another Holy Cave and is considered to be one of the direct disciples of Mila-repa....I was able to convince him of my sincerity and as a result he initiated me into this esoteric line as well as conferred upon me their authority, after his instructions, of being able to pass these teachings on to others who I feel worthy. The ritual consisted most of the repetition of endless mantras

and the throwing of much wheat, drinking of holy water, holy oil...it was very interesting, and I was honoured by the privilege for the Lamas who have been bringing him his daily hand full of barley and cup of yak's milk have never been able to really contact him....This hermit has never laid down to sleep in all those years...He is 65 and looks 40— mind very keen and in all around good health.[37]

I got tired and breathless as Theos' story unfolded. You say you convinced him of your sincerity?

"Indeed I did."

But early in the letter I just quoted, you said, "all sorts of things had to be done around the corners so to speak in order to impress them with the fact that I was a Buddhist, and this disguise I have had to hold all the time."

Theos cleared his throat. "I was writing to a professor. Scientific detachment is important in academia."

So you lied to the professor? Or was your Buddhism a lie?

"I meant to remain objective...but after all I saw, all I learned, all that happened to me here..."

Did you begin to feel like a reincarnated lama?

Theos sighed. "Sometimes yes, sometimes no."

You don't know? From all I've read of yours, heard about you, I can't get a handle on the contradictions of your personality. You said in a diary entry you were a polo player among the British, a cosmopolitan among the Tibetan nobility, and a lama among the lamas.

"So I was. A man may be many things. Your friends have stopped at that farmhouse. You can rest for a while there. We'll leave sleeping contradictions lie."

Pemba, YD, and Elizabeth had stopped at a house where a big fuzzy dog was chained in the courtyard. Was this one of the fierce mastiffs that guard peasants' homes? He didn't look fierce, but he wasn't especially friendly. No barking or snarling, but no tail wagging either; a serious watch dog.

The fieldstone farmhouse was surrounded by a low wall with an inner courtyard. Inside was a second wall on which a big pot of marigolds bloomed. In the courtyard a nun pumped a treadle sewing machine. The farmer who greeted us was slender, very tanned. He wore jeans, plaid shirt, and vest. He would have looked comfortable on an Iowa farm with a John Deere baseball cap. However, I'm sure he would be amazed by Iowa sized farms, the machinery used on them, and especially the pancake-flatness of the great plains.

We were welcomed into the one main room of the home in which most of the family's possessions hung from the rafters. The kitchen was across the small courtyard. The farmer offered us fresh shredded yak cheese which tasted like sharp cheddar. A couple of shy children watched us with solemn faces and round, curious eyes. I was reminded of Rinchen Dolma's description of when, as a child, she first saw an Englishman, Sir Charles Bell, the Tibetologist.

> A luncheon party was given...at Tsarong House...and I [was] thrilled to see Sir Charles who was said to have a red face, golden hair and a nose like a kettlespout. He was the first European we had seen and everybody peeped at him from every direction, whispering and giggling. His cook came ahead of him to prepare a chicken, because his health did not allow him to eat Tibetan food. His cook also made some buns which we were dying to eat, but until the party was over nobody would give us one.[38]

Another half hour of slow walking brought us to the first meditation cave chapel which contained a statue of Buddha, the usual butter lamps, a few offerings, very little additional space. The view from a tiny walled balcony was vertiginous but exhilarating. In the foreground, stood another mountain with a stone fence meandering around it, enclosing a large pasture. The long valley lay below. In the far distance, rows of mountains became ever paler blue and lavender, their snow crowns disappearing into the heavens.

By now we were ready to picnic on the box lunches we had brought. Warm jackets came off and water bottles came out. We found places to sit beside the trail, trying to avoid thistles and sheep dung. As a stone shifted under me I put my hand out to steady myself. "OW!" I yelped. The tip of a finger felt as it if had been bitten. I put it in my mouth.

BK said, "You touched a stinging nettle. That plant there." I looked carefully at the offending weed and saw sharp little spikes covering the leaves. My finger tingled for the next thirty-six hours. I will forever have respect for nettles. "Tradition has it that Milarepa mediated here for twelve years during which time he ate nothing but nettle soup," BK said.

Taking my finger out of my mouth, I said, "Sounds like a twelve year case of world class heart burn."

"If nettles are boiled long enough the spikes get soft. The soup is supposed to be bitter but nutritious, full of iron and vitamins," Mark informed me.

After lunch Rinchen Dolma walked along with me. "Look up there." I looked up toward the top of the mountain—which is not a very tall one as mountains go in this country, but, as I gasped for breath, it looked formidable to me. "There are meditation caves up, near the top. Do you see them?"

"Are you saying people climb all the way up there?"

"Oh, yes. They take a little food and water and stay three hours or three days or three weeks or three months. Very serious monks meditate three years, three months, three weeks, three day and three hours."

Heinrich joined us. As a serious mountaineer, this is his element. "Monks used to do that. I doubt they're allowed to any more."

I measured the distance of the meditation caves from where we were, keeping in mind that the exceptional clarity of the air makes distant places seem closer than they actually are. That would be some climb.

"Oh, we Tibetans can climb anywhere," Rinchen Dolma said with a twinkle of pride. "Some Germans can climb too," she added giving Heinrich a teasing smile.

"Thank you, Rinchen Dolma. You're thinking of our day here with Jigme, aren't you?"

"Yes. That was a lovely day like this, though earlier in the summer. Do you remember it was very windy that day?"

"It dried the sweat. Jigme and I scrambled up like mountain goats."

"Yes, you did, but I remember struggling, holding onto shrubs and looking straight down. I thought the wind would surely tear me and the shrubs right off that narrow path and I'd go tumbling down. You and Jigme were far ahead of me and I didn't want to give up. I remember crying from fear and exhaustion."

"Crying? Oh, I'm sorry. I didn't know."

"I didn't want you to know. I asked Jigme not to tell you when he came down to help me. I was so cold and frightened, I would never have made it to that peaceful little cave that enchanted us so much if he hadn't taken my hand and pulled me over the face of the cliff. I said a prayer of gratitude for having such a kind husband."

In your long skirt and simple shoes, I don't know how you did it.

Alexandra was waiting for us as the track made a hairpin turn. Her presence was unexpected because she did not write of coming here. "You're right, I didn't come here," she said, reading my mind, of course. "But I struggled up and over many mountains tracks like this."

"Yes, I'm sure you did on your way to Lhasa, as did I," Heinrich said, "But you didn't really have to."

"Heinrich, you could have stayed, snug and safe in your prisoner-of-war camp in India, and I could have settled down in a boring little vine-covered cottage in France when I was told I wouldn't be allowed to visit Lhasa. And aren't we glad we chose our difficult journeys?"

"But you were in disguise and could have followed the regular pilgrim road, however, by your own account, you preferred to strike out across the unknown territory in southeastern Tibet just because it had never been crossed by a European. So you created your own difficulties."

110

"Who doesn't?" Alexandra asked.

The steep mountain track was difficulty enough for me. The pasture land gave way to scrubby, rocky hillside. Along the trail I came upon a sheep or two, a goat nosing along, looking for edible plants. A yak stood in a clump of low trees staring past me with bovine indifference. Another yak lay ruminating—which is bovine meditation, isn't it?—in his own little cave under a jutting rock.

I went into a cave chapel with a brand new Buddha statue. The smell of yak butter lamps mingled with the pottery studio-like smell of wet clay for the new statues had only recently dried enough to be painted. Along the sides of the chapel were equally new standing statues of bodhasativas clothed in gaudy brocades, draped with kathag. The highest point I reached was a new chorten, so far merely raw concrete. Chorten is Tibetan for the Sanskrit *stupa*, a religious structure that is a three dimensional mandala.

A whole community of pilgrims, mostly monks and nuns, were encamped near the chorten. Gradually our entire group arrived. Pemba learned from the pilgrims that a rinpoche was in residence at the chapel just above the chorten. A rinpoche is a lama who is known to be a reincarnation. Some highly evolved souls, Buddhists believe, freely choose, when the soul is in the limbo-like afterworld entered immediately after death, not to escape the wheel of reincarnation which their highly evolved state would allow, but to return to Earth in order to serve others and aid them on their spiritual journey. The most famous rinpoche is, of course, the Dalai Lama. According to Harrer, in the past a thousand or more rinpoches were recognized.

"We can visit the rinpoche," Pemba announced after making inquiries.

BK loves such serendipity. He and the others went. I was blissed out with the view from the chorten and barely noticed their leaving. YD, BK's partner, stayed with me; part of his job is to keep track of stray group members, but he was less interested in religious ceremonies than BK. YD is Thai and grew up a Buddhist, but not of the Tibetan persuasion.

A soft silence filled the air even though about a hundred people were in the area. As at Sera, I was enchanted by the absence of the noise of a be-gadgeted first world country.

"First?" said Theos. "It's hubris to claim America is 'first.' This came first! This quiet, this natural peacefulness."

Oh, Theos, if you weren't a phantom, I'd hug you. You're so right.

During the hour I sat on the stone wall small events took place around me. Just beyond and below, a round-topped mountain rose out of the field that would otherwise sweep down into the valley. A path wound down from the nearby encampment and then up and around the small mountain. A procession of monks and nuns were like a string of jewels against the gray-green of the sparse vegetation. The procession looked like a scene from a Bertolucci movie. They walked single file to the mountain top where they gathered in small groups. Some continued on to a meadow fifty yards below my perch and stopped at a stone shrine before which they prostrated several times, then wandered away in various directions.

The mountain is a sky burial site although no burial is taking place today. The highest lamas are mummified and other important lamas are cremated. In a fuel-poor country, cremation is impractical. Most people are taken for sky burial to places in the mountains where special priests perform the rite. The flesh is flayed into small strips that are fed to vultures which—I've read, though it sounds like an exaggeration— sit on rocks and branches of the low trees, awaiting the signal to gorge themselves.

"Not true," said Theos. He sat cross-legged on the stone wall near me. "The butchers I watched had a boy with a whip to beat back the birds. You know, I saw a sky burial near Shigatse."

"Excuse me, Theos," Rinchen Dolma said softly, "I think she's remembering my description. When I watched a sky burial at Sera Monastery the birds did, indeed, wait. And there were hundreds of them. I was a young girl—not a child—I was old enough to remember and understand. I can still see that huge, silent flock with their bright eyes and sharp beaks watching as the men flayed the flesh from the three corpses lying face down on a slab of rock."

Thank you, Rinchen Dolma. So, to go on, eventually even the bones are crushed and, in some descriptions, are mixed with tsampa. In other descriptions the crushed bones are mixed with the viscera and brain to make them palatable to the carrion birds.

"That's right." Theos agreed. "I think the ritual is a little different in different places."

Every Tibetan traveler writes about sky burial. I think it's often related as a frightful barbarity or told for the titillation value.

"Well, you're doing it too," Theos nudged me with a wink.

Touché. I would be remiss if I didn't. Wouldn't I?

"I think you would be remiss if you didn't point out that the body without the soul is nothing and its return to the cycle of being is inevitable," Theos preached as if he had assumed the lama's robe.

"Besides," said scientific-minded Heinrich, "sky burial is an efficient solution to the problem of what to do with bodies in a country where the ground is so rocky and hard that graves would be difficult to dig except in the precious river plain. They can't use the only arable land for cemeteries."

"Right," Theos agreed. "I like the way your mind works, Henry—"

"Heinrich, please."

"Oh, sorry. As I was about to explain, the body's substances re-enter the cycle of life, first feeding the birds, and when they die and their bodies disintegrate they return to the earth. Or the birds are eaten by wild animals and there is another step before return. The cycle of life whirls like the prayer wheels. If you think about it as I do, preserving bodies in leaden coffins or stone mausoleums is unnatural, even ghoulish."

"Theos, we have a new concept now, called ecology," Heinrich said. "Everything is interdependent, nothing is lost, only transformed forever and ever."

"Tell me about ecology, Heinrich," Theos said.

They walked away, leaving YD and me on the wall near the chorten. A workman approached and climbed onto the first level of structure. He had a tank of water strapped to his back which had a hose attachment and a pump device and began to water down the new concrete. Two tiny monks, about seven or eight years old, who had been wandering about watched the worker. They whispered together, plotting mischief like any other boys that age. They threw pebbles at the man's feet then ducked out of sight around the edge of the chorten. The man looked around and may have seen the boys, but he ignored them. Then the bigger and bolder of the two boys tossed another pebble. The man quickly squirted some water in the boy's direction, causing gales of laughter.

For about twenty minutes the boys dashed around the chorten, occasionally tossing a pebble, once grabbing the man's hat off his head. He aimed the squirts of water with precision, barely sprinkling the smaller boy since he often hung back and watched as his slightly older friend teased the workman relentlessly. When the older boy's cloak was entirely soaked he took it off and flung it on the wall, revealing a sleeveless yellow satin brocade tunic. He simply couldn't stop teasing the man, who never once lost his patience nor said anything to the boys, even when he grabbed back his hat. The bigger boy continued laughing although his undershirt clung to him as water dripped off his nose, ears and elbows. YD and I smiled, fascinated by the man's tolerance and his poker faced retaliation.

The man's attitude toward the boys was entirely unlike what I would expect from people I know. Americans are less indulgent of children than people in many other cultures. The first half of Rinchen Rinchen Dolma's autobiography, *Daughter of Tibet*, is about growing up, a child from a noble family orphaned young and taken under the guardianship of her older sister's husband, the wealthy and modern-thinking Tsarong Shappé, who I've mentioned as Theos' and Heinrich's host in Lhasa. She was the first Tibetan girl to study outside Tibet, in Darjeeling, where she learned English. In school there, she chose to be called Mary and met her future husband.

As a noble child, Rinchen Dolma enjoyed a number of privileges other children did not.

"I admit," Rinchen Dolma said perching on the edge of the chorten, "As a child I was rather lazy about walking and often had to be carried up and down the steps of the Tsarong house. The water carrier used to wait at the gate and take me up the two long staircases on my return from school." She paused with a far away smile, remembering a very different time and place. "All the children had to sweep the school and school yard but noble children sent servants to sweep for them."

But your rank didn't save you from physical punishment at school.

"No, no, not at all. Once I had not completed my writing exercise when suddenly the master's window was thrown open and we knew he was going to check our work before sending us to lunch. Each student had to show his writing and when my turn came I got hold of somebody else's good writing and showed this. The master looked me in the face and told me to continue writing after lunch. I was so frightened that I...did not return to school, hoping that the master might forget about me. But next morning, when everybody was reading loudly, he called me and said that the most naughty daughter of the Tsarongs could not be controlled until she had been given a good thrashing. He called two boys to hold me down by the arms and legs, in the usual way, but I told him that I could take the whipping without being held and lay on the ground and pulled down my knickers. After four or five lashes I jumped up and ran home. Some boys were sent to catch me, but I successfully hid from them in a baker's dark shop."[40]

I remember, too, that you wrote about coming home from Darjeeling accompanied by servants. Sometimes you decided to ride your pony through a field, chasing antelopes instead of staying on track.

Rinchen Dolma laughed her soft, young laugh. "Yes, I did that. I loved galloping on my pony."

You slowed the journey, but you say you were never scolded. Was that because they were your servants?

"Well, yes, of course."

And the man on the stupa never said a word to the bothersome little monks.

"Oh, he respects them. They had a nice game just now. Why shouldn't they?"

You're quite right, Rinchen Dolma. I could have used some of that man's patience when my daughters were small.

We lapsed into silence. I watched a yak wander up the path just below my perch. Suddenly a middle-aged monk rushed out of his tent which was beside the path and began shouting at the yak. What a contrast to the patient workman.

Rinchen Dolma moved aside as Theos rejoined us. Ah, Theos, I'm glad you're back. You know I didn't come to meditate in a religious sense, but I've been meditating in my own way. You're the theology student, tell me something about the dichotomy of Lhalung Paldor who killed the king and the Buddhist prescription against killing.

"People are human and they do what they must."

That's not enough of an answer. Maybe I'll ask Alexandra, she studied theology too.

Theos immediately began talking as if he were afraid Alexandra would appear and preempt him. "Think of this: the Tibetans eat meat although people in the West think that to be Buddhist means to be vegetarian. Some of the most holy lamas avoid eating meat, but the country has a very limited variety of foods. For the hard work most people have to do, they need meat. So they eat yak meat mostly, and rarely chicken, fish, goat or sheep. The theological idea is that one yak's life will feed many, but one chicken or fish will feed only one or two. They compromise and do what has to be done. The same practical view explains why the hermit, Lhalung Paldor, was driven to kill the king which was not a random and unprovoked act."

Alexandra arrived, unable to let Theos have the final word on the matter. She said, "Let me put it in Western terms. Wouldn't someone have been a great hero if he had assassinated Hitler? And wouldn't he have saved countless lives? Here in Tibet people admire the Khampas who fought so hard against the Chinese invasion."

"We humans have an instinct to fight for what we love even if it means killing—no matter how much we abhor killing," Theos put in.

"Buddhism," Alexandra added with finality, "like other religions, is about learning to direct your energies and instincts toward understanding and compassion."

My companions returned from their audience with the rinpoche, the afternoon was melting away. As we were about to go back down to our van, Elizabeth collected three tiny Tibetan women who had walked all the way from Lhasa that morning and were now going to walk back. They were small, slender, tough, possibly in their fifties as we were, maybe younger. Their weathered skin made them look worn but they were hearty and smiling. They communicated, mostly in sign language as they walked part of the way down through the pastures with us, often taking our hands to help us over a few stepping stones in a stream and down steep parts of the path.

Going down was, of course, far easier than going up had been. The pellucid late afternoon light was honey-toned. The valley stretched below me and the cave-riddled cliff loomed above. I reached the van before some of the others and I decided to walk alone down the road prolonging my experience of the countryside. My phantom guides accompanied me in silence. They had each written with their own kind of eloquence about the beauty of this country. I understood Alexandra's choice to prolong her journey by taking an unnecessarily long route just to see countryside that she believed no European had seen before. Much too soon the van stopped to pick me up. I would like to have walked to Lhasa like the Tibetan pilgrim women, even it if took all night.

Children on stairs watching Lhamo

RAMOCHE

King Srongsten Gampo, he with the mustache like cat's whiskers and two favorite wives, was responsible for building not only the Jokhang, but also Ramoche monastery which houses the statue of Buddha brought as dowry by Gyasa, his Chinese wife. Sometimes called "the little Jokhang," it is even more modest than the Jokhang. It stands in the crowded northeast of the city and is the second most holy structure in Lhasa. Our van moved slowly through the busy, shop-lined street in the middle of which were knife sharpeners, a dealer in used clothing, peddlers of apples and pears. The atmosphere is more authentic and less tourist oriented than the Barkor area.

"Oh, my goodness!" Theos was standing in the street as I got out of the van. He waved his hand at the street. "I told you that Ramoche is situated just at the edge of the town—"

As you said, 'the way that leads there offers an interesting spectacle of Tibetan life....the shops show how the various crafts are carried on.' It's still true. Look at those newly made, bronze temple ornaments gleaming in the sunshine.

"I also reported that the streets were filled with donkeys, yaks, dogs, sheep, goats, horses, Lamas, beggars, men, women and children."

You see, Theos, it's built up but otherwise it's much the same. Just more people and fewer animals.

"You don't understand. Where we're standing now, in front of the monastery—which by the way looks quite different. I suppose you're going to tell me—"

Yes, a great deal was destroyed.

"Damn their eyes!" He stormed about in a fury for a while then returned and said, "You didn't mention the dying beggar."

Waddell appeared striding through the throng. He glared me rather fiercely. "See here, dear lady, if you're writing about how it used to be, don't stop with the picturesque. Tell them the whole truth. You say you're not one of those soft-headed romantics who think everything past was perfect. I told you about the excrement. Go on, quote what Theos wrote about the beggar."

It's not at all nice.

"Nice! Nice?! What honest writer thinks about nice. A woman, that's what. Men tell the truth, women worry about whether something is nice." Waddell was never more disdainful.

Damnit, Colonel, Theos' description is so ugly.

Theos supported Waddell, "I know people are squeamish and—what's that phrase you used? 'Politically correct?' Well, the whole truth is never politically incorrect."

Waddell growled now at Theos, "Dear boy, you can't be *that* naive. People don't like the truth, certainly not the WHOLE truth. The streets of Lhasa were smelly, festering, medieval, and in some ways, rotten places. They claimed they had a system of storage so that there were no famines in Tibet before the Chinese took over, yet people did starve...and died even more horrible deaths. If you're not squeamish about the truth, give his whole quote."

I've had a moment to recover. I will, Colonel, but first I want to say that I will not apologize for caring about niceness. It may be more superficial than goodness but it underlies civility and sensitivity to others. The world very much needs more niceness.

Waddell started to turn away with a "Hurrrumph." Here's Theos' story of the beggar.

"You pass a *mani* (sacred wall) about a hundred yards in length with the usual throng of beggars squatting beneath its sacred emblems. I do not believe there is a place in the world which can compare with Tibet for its herds of dejected travelling mendicants who pass through this life clothed in tatters and with begging bowls in their hands. Mendicancy is considered a respectable profession in this land, though the lot of the beggars at best is far from an enviable one, to judge from the ones you see, with scarce a real flicker of life among them.

Our jaunt was not without its pathetic touch. We joined a rapidly increasing crowd, attracted to the sight of a human being taking his last breaths while prostrated on the kerb, with almost the entire calf of one leg eaten off and the heel of the other foot gone; and there was all the gore that colors such a scene. It appears that one of the dogs had become a little hungry and helped himself ..."[41]

"Well, we did try to help him but he thought people would pity him and give him a coin or two. He wouldn't hear of being moved," Theos said.

It's a terrible story, Theos. I'd really like to change the subject to the monastery. You mentioned a thick row of trees and a stand of hollyhocks. That's all gone.

After remembering the scene with the beggar, Theos was in a bad mood. "Everything's a disaster. The Chinese are like that man-eating dog."

Waddell was being tough on both of us today. He said, "You might look around and see that no beggars are being eaten alive by hungry dogs. In fact, I don't see any beggars at all. Anyone who cares about human beings has got to call that an improvement."

Theos replied, "It's very well, Colonel, to improve the lot of the least of men, but when the best of men, the most learned and advanced, were murdered and their books destroyed, it's hardly a quid pro quo."

This did not improve Waddell's sour mood, "Furthermore, it's good to see some work being done here. When I saw it I noted that it was 'in a very neglected almost ruinous condition.'[42] The Tibetans, themselves, were not always perfect stewards of their heritage."

Indeed, the courtyard was cluttered with new paving stones in piles where restoration work proceeded slowly. To the left of the courtyard a plain two-story dormitory to house monks was being constructed.

We left the bright, sunny day and entered a short passageway that felt like an ancient cave. The assembly hall was not as big as that at the Jokhang. The smell of burning butter permeated the building. A few devout older people, and even some younger ones, circumambulated the hall. I was reminded of similarly ancient churches tucked into narrow streets in Rome, Florence, and Venice.

Ramoche is home to the Gyuto monks who are famous for their deep, sonorous chanting. Pemba had learned when the monks would be in chapel and we had timed our visit in order to hear them. After a few minutes about twenty-five monks took their places on the benches and pulled their heavy cloaks around themselves. Most of them were middle aged, the first group of mature men that we had seen.

"Oh my, oh my, oh my..." Theos muttered as he wedged himself beside me.

Yes, Theos, I know. The hall must have been full to overflowing when you witnessed a special Tantric ceremony here. Please let me listen and compare what I hear to what you wrote.

> The chants, begun by the head chorister, who filled the room
> with the unending roll of thunder in the heavens, were
> picked up by the eight hundred Lamas only to be relieved
> by the tinkling of their bells, for every Lama had his bell...[43]

Only the "head chorister," as Theos called him, had a bell, but there
were a couple of cymbals. The leader, a distinguished man who looked
about fifty with a roughedly handsome face, had the air of an important
personage. His cowl was up around his ears, his head was covered with
a stubble of black hair.

I was fascinated and amused by a fairly young monk whose profile I
could see very clearly. He seemed to be working his protuberant lips
more self-consciously and extravagantly than the others—he had a
repertoire of facial expressions to make a mime proud. The voices were
baso profundo, the lowest tones the human voice can make, amazing
sounds that rumbled like simmering lava. I do not have the musical ear
or training to understand how difficult it is to make and control such
sounds. Later Pat, a musician, said, "They produce two tones at the same
time." She talked about the physiology of the larynx and said, "Jimi
Hendrix could do the same thing."

The monks chanted for fifteen minutes, then a young monk came in
with a big thermos of tea. All the chanters brought out their own red lac-
quered bowls. They held the steaming tea until another monk came in
with a container of tsampa. He ladled three spoons full into each bowl.
The monks dipped their fingers into the bowls and began to kneed the
tsampa into dough balls. Tsampa mixed with buttered, salted tea has for
ages been a staple of the Tibetan diet.

Theos whispered. "I grew very fond of Tibetan tea. The butter and salt
are whipped into it making it more soup than tea. And tsampa balls are
very delicious because barley flour is naturally sweet."

As the monks began another period of chanting, I shifted positions
because my ankles ached and my bottom was cold. In this ancient room,
my ears filled with some of the most remarkable sounds human voices

can make. But I have to admit, I was more bored than interested. Theos was moved by such chanting, which, of course, was more impressive from eight hundred than twenty-eight voices, but I don't know what he really felt. I wish he had written more about the emotional and intellectual states religious ceremonies induced in him. But he was not a very good writer, really. He told what he saw and did so using the clichés of the 1930s.

"What do you mean I'm not a very good writer?" Theos hissed in my ear.

I thought you were meditating.

"Your insulting thought interrupted me!"

"Stop, both of you." Alexandra, sitting on the other side of me, leaned forward to face us both. "Your attitudes set up bad vibrations here. The language of ecstasy really got it's modern punch after psychodelics and the Beats. You can't expect Theos to write like Allen Ginsberg or Timothy Leary. Let him go back to his meditations."

"You've ruined the morning for me." Theos stalked out.

"These men are too touchy," Alexandra gave me a woman-to-woman smile. "They jump on your back for being nice, but when you tell a plain truth about them..." She opened her hands in a what-can-you-do gesture.

Alexandra, help me understand. I love listening to classical music, why can't I relate to this chanting?

"You're limited by how cultured you are," Alexandra said pointedly. "Understanding your own culture and its arts has been important to you, but one culture doesn't prepare you to understand another. Simpler people would understand more intuitively than you do...or people who have studied this culture far more deeply—like Theos and I did."

I'd like to be open to the ritual, but some tide constantly washes me back into my own ways of thinking and hearing.

"You're closed off," Alexandra said like a school marm. "Being reminded that you're not so open and multi-cultural isn't very pleasant, is it? You've admitted you don't understand prayer...I'll say this for you, knowing your ignorance won't stop eating at you. You'll go home and read and read...but your understanding will remain limited."

Thank you very much, Cassandra David-Neel.

Alexandra shrugged. "I've been called worse names."

When the chanting ended Pemba told us, "Come, we can meet the Abbot."

We went into a simple room on the upper story of the building and were directed to take seats on a bench all in a row like school children. The Abbot's reception room seemed to have the only telephone in the monastery. Various people came in to use it while we were there. I noted that it was a touch tone phone and remembered reading that developing countries skip entire layers of technological development. They leap from abacus to computer, from horse back messengers to fiberoptics.

A young monk served us bowls of buttered tea. I lifted mine to my mouth and made a pretense of sipping. The smell was revolting. Yes, Alexandra was right, I'm not as open to new experiences as I wish I were.

The day proved to be one for music appreciation lessons. Pemba gave us a lagniappe, an unexpected gift, a treat. "Pemba says they're performing an opera in his village," BK told us as we left Ramoche. "We can go if you'd like to see it. Or if someone would rather not go, the van can take you directly back to the Holiday Inn. What do you think?"

We were unanimously delighted by the idea of visiting Pemba's village and seeing a traditional opera, called a *lhamo*. Before Lhasa spread to fill the whole valley Pemba's village would have been outside the city gates. Now the village is an enclave just off the road from the Holiday Inn to the center of Lhasa.

Pemba lead us into a passage between high whitewashed walls. We entered a warren of alleys with openings into courtyards, dead ends, and no signs, numbers or other indications of where we were. Villages all over the world naturally evolve with twisted little streets that follow the whims of builders or the lay of the land. On the one hand such streets strike fear into the heart of Midwesterners like myself; on the other, they are intriguing and mysterious, promising glimpses of different ways of life.

I grew up in that part of the Midwest where surveyors laid out the entire state in one mile squares. To this day I have an intuitive knowledge of north, south, east and west and a clear mental picture of a mile. The Midwestern gridded landscape fits the predominantly Protestant, conservative farmers who settled the land. They were repressed, very predictable, dependable, mostly honest, unexciting. Square. For the curious among us who chafed at this kind of physical and mental gridlock, the long straight highways made escape to more exotic places as easy as following the road. Curiosity had brought me half way around the world.

Pemba took us down passageways and around corners. We were drawn toward the sound of drum beats and high pitched female voices. Unexpectedly, we stepped into a crowded courtyard which was shaded by a canvas awning and cloistered with two-storied houses. The opera was being performed in the center of the courtyard. In front of us was a small monastery that looked no different than the other houses. Several monks were sitting on an upper veranda, the equivalent of box seats.

People of all ages had gathered for the opera. They made space for us, some offered bits of cardboard so we didn't have to sit directly on the packed earth. Many children, rosy cheeked and bright eyed, look at us curiously. They didn't point or speak loudly, even the restless ones who shoved at each other weren't disruptive. No embarrassed or over-protective parent interfered.

Lhamo is a folk opera with traditional costumes and masks. This lhamo was titled *The Chinese Princess*. Characters included the princess who marries a king of Tibet, messengers who bring Buddhism from India, an entourage of pretty young women (including Pemba's sister), a wizard or Father Time figure with long white hair, a clown with a dog's head mask, the king and his retinue, etc. The royal characters wore very intricately sewn brocades and silks in a dazzle of red, blue, green, and gold with silk tassels at many points. The men wore traditional embroidered felt boots with upturned toes which peeked out as they stomped and whirled. Sleeves of the men's costumes were long enough to hide their hands; they became wing-like when the dancer swooped. We could have used a Playbill with a precis of the plot which was as convoluted as any opera by Verdi or Rossini.

I heard Theos mutter, "I supposed *you* could call it opera—"

Of course it's opera. It's drama with music and dance and it's also classical.

"Well, I called it drama." I sensed that both Theos and Heinrich were sitting behind me.

"So do I," Heinrich said. "Daily performances went on for a whole month in the summer," Theos added.

I've read that there were troops of strolling players rather like the ones who visited Elsinor and took Prince Hamlet's advice on what story to present, how to act, trying not to 'saw the air' too much and so on.

"I believe that was true out in the countryside." Heinrich said, "but not here in Lhasa. The groups I saw were, as you see here, people who have other everyday work. They were tireless and wonderful."

"I found it rather boring, actually," Theos said.

"Didn't you see the satirical dramas?" Heinrich asked.

"Not that I remember."

"You'd remember. The Tibetans really love to laugh. They enjoy comedy more than any group I know," Heinrich said.

"Absolutely," Theos agreed. "Didn't I remark that I saw Tsarong literally roll on the floor, overcome with glee, at some joke? And whole rooms of lamas making the rafters rumble when they laughed? But I didn't see any funny dramas."

You missed something delightful. Here's how Heinrich described it.

> One of the seven groups of actors...is famous for its parodies....One could not but be astonished at their frankness. It is a proof of the good humor and sanity of the people that they can make fun of their own weakness and

even of their religious institutions. They go so far as to give
a performance of the Oracle, with dance and trance and all,
which brings down the house. Men appear dressed as nuns
and imitate in the drollest fashion the fervour of women begging for alms. When monks and nuns begin to flirt together
on the stage, no one can stop laughing and tears roll down
the cheeks of the sternest abbots in the audience.[44]

"I wish I'd seen that one," Theos said. "What I remember is long lunches
that seemed to have a hundred courses and gallons of *chang* (barley
beer) while all day performances of the religious stories were acted in
the courtyard. The common people crowded around the sides, just as
they are here in this little village. This very lhamo was done—same costumes, same masks, same whining women's voices."

Shush, shush, guys. I want to watch this. The phantoms got up and
wandered out into the village. Instead of the opera, I found myself
watching Pemba holding a child. "His niece," Sharon whispered to me.
I thought that by bringing us here, Pemba was displaying "his" Americans to his neighbors; at the same time, he was showing the Americans
his friends and family. Perhaps he was telling us, "See, I'm from a nice
neighborhood."

Pemba is medium height and build; his features are as gentle as his
soft voice. A man in his late twenties, he spoke good, but very accented
English that was sometimes difficult to understand. He was serious
natured but sometimes he made a gentle joke. He had completed the
guide's training course but he wasn't sure he would remain a tour guide.
He had had other jobs and might yet go into a different occupation, or
so he told us. Pemba was quickly at ease with the Tibetans we met,
whether farmers or pilgrims at Yerpa, monks in the monasteries, children anywhere. He knew the iconography of the statues and paintings
in the monasteries and he didn't talk about politics except for an occa-
sional mention of the Cultural Revolution.

Later I asked Pemba if he had ever heard of Tsarong Shappé and if I could find out if Tsarong House still stood. No he had never heard the name Tsarong, he didn't know anything about Tsarong House. From the book by English teacher Catriona Bass, who was in Lhasa in the mid-80s when Pemba would have been in school, I understand that only a few bright Tibetan children (boys) could manage to get modern (i.e., Chinese) education. Any recent history taught in schools was what the Chinese chose to impart: how terrible the "medieval" conditions in Tibet were, how much better off Tibet is now that it has been "liberated", and how Chinese have brought all good modern things here including, of course, the Chinese brand of Communist education.

Pemba did not know the word "shappé" which would be roughly translated as Cabinet Minister, Tibet's highest lay government position. Three of my ghost guides knew Tsarong Shappé well. He was certainly a very important figure in Tibet from the 1920s through the 1950s. I think I could assume he was as important a political figure in Tibet as, say Nelson Rockefeller or Hubert Humphrey was in the United States, yet Pemba, an intelligent, decently educated young Tibetan, had learned nothing about him or even the office he held.

I was caught in a web of contradictory feelings. Heinrich noted a couple of times in *Return to Tibet* that in 1982 restoration of monasteries was mostly sham, a show put on for the first handful of tourists allowed to visit the country. Now, clearly at Ramoche and the other monasteries restorations are taking place, however slowly. This performance of lhamo was not being given for tourists. It was proof of a degree of religious freedom. Again I can only compare the Tibetan situation to that of Native Americans or perhaps Australian aborigines—people who, after periods of massacre, remain marginalized by descendants of the Europeans who colonized their countries. Their native languages are not taught and much of their history is lost except in the writings of the first Europeans who came in contact with them, and thus are seen from an imposed perspective.

Likewise, almost all that we know about the cultures of Central and South America comes from the writings of their conquerors. Inca, Aztec,

Mayan and many other cultures have vanished. However, in several parts of the world, the end of the 20th century is marked by a resurgence of ethnic pride—a two-edged sword. Some Islamic countries have regressed into a repressive fundamentalism.

Perhaps every era has been a time of great change and the present only seems so restless and dynamic because modern communications make us aware of turmoil around the globe. The Tibetans inhabit a special niche because the Shangri-La myth added an overlay of romance as their plight has unfolded in the media and because they are so ably represented by the Dalai Lama. However, relatively few people know much about the culture that has been destroyed. Young Tibetans like Pemba are ignorant of their history and most of his counterparts in the disapora have never seen their homeland and cannot know it's uniqueness firsthand.

NORBULINKA AND TSERPU

On a free afternoon I walked the short distance from the Holiday Inn to Norbulinka, the Dalai Lama's summer residence. I strolled past the Chinese markets along one of the busiest entry roads into Lhasa—a very different approach than the one Theos described.

> The park is a little over a mile beyond the city. The countryside surrounding the place...is a jungle swamp of trees which forms a dense shaded boulevard for about a quarter of a mile to the entrance of a typical Chinese design, carved and painted in the royal colors of the native faith. This led to the old palace, which has been the home of the past Dalai Lamas but the last, who built a new one for himself. His palace is situated at the back of the large enclosure surrounded by a wall of solid rock of about twelve feet high. I have no idea of its exact size, but I should say that it would require a full day to walk about its spacious grounds, that is, if you did it rather briskly. This great enclosure holds innumerable isolated houses, extensive stables, endless gar-

Heinrich Harrer

dens, runways for favorite animals, such as tiger, leopards, bears, monkeys and deer, and a very large bird-cage for peacocks and several varieties of birds with which I am not familiar.

There were also endless winding paths, perfumed by flowering gardens....

We dismounted outside the rear entrance which leads directly to the new palace...a short lane bordered with towering trees led from this entrance to the entrance of the patio of the last Dalai Lama's palace. Beyond this entrance... there appeared the even more impressive vision of a modest dwelling, its gilded roof blazing in the sun...only the roof over the Dalai Lama's tomb at the Potala surpassed this in beauty.[44]

I not only did not pass through willow groves, but I also had to use the front entrance. Instead of the garrisons of soldiers both Heinrich and Theos described guarding the entrance, I was met by a ticket taker and two large, ugly, gaudily painted snow lion statues draped with kathag. I paused inside the gate wondering whether to go straight ahead or to follow the path to the right. Then I realized that to go right would mean walking counterclockwise, so I went straight ahead assuming that in Tibet everything, even a walk in the park, should be done clockwise.

Heinrich galloped up on a horse which he jumped off and led along behind us as we strolled. I was not surprised to find him here since he came here often when he tutored the Dalai Lama.

During the period when the current Dalai Lama had not been discovered, Theos saw an unused residence. Heinrich's descriptions added depth to Theos' recollections.

...I had many opportunities to admire the beautiful grounds and the splendid fruit trees and conifers which had been brought from all parts of Tibet. A host of gardeners looked after the flowers and trees and kept the paths in order...In the middle of the park is the private garden of the Living Buddha, surrounded by a high, yellow wall. It has two gates strongly guarded by soldiers through which, apart from His Holiness, only the abbots appointed as his guardians may pass. Not even Cabinet Ministers are admitted. Through the foliage one can glimpse the golden roofs of temples but the cry of the peacocks is the only sound which escapes to the outside world....At short intervals there are dog-kennels built into the wall, whose savage, long-haired tenants bark when anyone comes too near. The yak-hair leashes prevent the dogs from attacking, but their hoarse growling sounds a discordant note in this peaceful world. Afterwards, when I was privileged to enter the secret garden through the gates in the yellow wall, I made friends, as far as one could, with these rough fellows.[45]

"I'm glad they're maintaining Norbulinka as a park—though maintaining is a little too active a verb for the general neglect here," Heinrich said looking into the wooded area beside the path. Straggly weeds pushed through a mat of fallen leaves under the trees and among fallen branches. The quiet was almost eerie. I turned to Heinrich, more grateful than ever for ghostly company.

I loved your chapter on tutoring the Dalai Lama here, building a movie theatre for him, and his desire to study Western subjects with you.

"He was always a boy to me, never a god-king."

You expressed that sweetly when you wrote about his passing you in his sedan chair on some official occasion.

Heinrich thought for a minute, calling up a memory of nearly fifty years ago. "Yes, he gave me a smile and my private thought was that he was congratulating himself on his little cinema, but I am sure that no one else thought as I did; though what could be more natural for a lonely fourteen-year-old boy? Then a look at the humble and rapturous face of my attendant reminded me that for everyone else except myself, he was not a lonely boy but a god."[46]

I know you agree with me that to be human is enough in this world, divinity is an idea—or wish—not a fact.

"We're certainly a minority in thinking that, worldwide."

Which doesn't mean we're wrong. And it didn't prevent you from being at home in a theocracy.

Heinrich walked along nodding in thought. "Yes, I was at home here." He pointed to a small chapel we were approaching. "You should go into that shrine."

Is it important?

"No, not really. But do go in, you'll see why."

I went into the shrine—a single room with statues, the usual murals on the wall, and nothing else except butter lamps and bowls of water on the altar. The two Tibetan men in civilian clothes at the entrance were, I supposed, caretakers. One followed me inside. He told me the name of the aspect of Buddha represented in main statue. He allowed me a moment to look at it then asked, "Where are you from?"

"America."

"America. Good. What city?"

"New York."

"New York is a very big city."

"Yes, very big."

"Much bigger than Lhasa?"

"Much, much bigger than Lhasa, but I like Lhasa very much."

I'd grown accustomed to Pemba's accent, although I didn't always understand everything he said, but this young man was more difficult to decipher; he hadn't had many tourists on whom to practice his English.

I suddenly became aware that the young man was watching the door. He seemed afraid of being overheard.

"Why did you come to Tibet?" he asked.

"To see Lhasa and the monasteries and the mountains and the country-side," I answered.

"Do you like Tibet?"

"Yes, very much."

"Tibet is not free."

"I know and I wish Tibet were free."

"We are not free to worship and they have destroyed the Dalai Lama's pictures. They tell lies about the Dalai Lama"

I nodded yes. "I know," I said.

"Last month soldiers went into homes and monasteries and destroyed pictures. There were protests at Ganden. Do you know Ganden monastery?"

"I know it's closed to tourists now."

He talked on, repeating his dissatisfactions. I don't know what else he said because I couldn't penetrate his accent. He talked quickly—a torrent of explanation. I felt his nervous tension as he kept glancing at the doorway hoping we would not be interrupted. At the same time, a paranoid part of me wondered if he was an undercover agent trying to get me to give him Dalai Lama pictures so he could arrest me and score points with the authorities for apprehending a subversive tourist. But he asked nothing of me except my attention. As long as I stood and listened he simply poured out, in a low hurried voice, his litany of unhappiness about Communists in Tibet. His monologue ended with, "Do you know what I am saying?"

"Yes."

"Will you tell Americans in New York about Tibet?"

"Yes, I will."

He smiled with satisfaction and pointed out the other deities in the murals. As I reached the door he told me much of Norbulinka was closed today, more was open on weekends, but I could walk around.

"*Tashi deleg*," I said.

I went out and found Heinrich waiting for me, still holding his horse's reins. "Was it an interesting shrine?" he asked with a knowing smile.

No, but the young man was. I wish I'd understood him better. I was somewhat uncomfortable.

"It was all right to listen to him, he needed to feel that people in the West know what's going on here."

I didn't understand more than a quarter of what he said to me. I can't even bear witness fully—

"You'll go home and do what you can do. I'll leave you in peace, I know that you enjoy solitary walks."

That's true. Thank you, Heinrich.

He mounted his horse and rode away. He was the right person in the right place at the right time—a man who never was overawed by the concept of divinity. Heinrich recognized the inherent nobleness of a boy of whom far more would be demanded than even his intense education could have prepared him to handle, yet he continues, in exile, to lead his people with the grace that has earned him the respect of the world.

I spent an hour wandering around, going into a couple more chapels and peering through the locked gate into the Dalai Lama's private garden. Again I was alone with an eerie silence where once paths would have been busy with gardeners, and lamas bustling to and fro on important errands.

At this time only one of the foremost reincarnated lamas can be visited in central Tibet. The Dalai Lama, of course, is living in Dharmsala, India; the former Pachen Lama's reincarnation is a matter of contention. The Karmapa, the reincarnated head of the Kagyud school of Tibetan Buddhism is also under dispute. One Karmapa is headquartered at Tserpu Monastery, approximately fifty miles from Lhasa and is recognized by the Chinese and the Tibetans in Tibet; but another Karmapa is living at Rumtek Monastery in Sikkim, India and is recognized by exiled members of his sect.

Perhaps both are "real" Karmapas. Tibetans have a tradition of multiple incarnations. For a Westerner who cannot believe in physical reincarnation, the idea of two simultaneous incarnations of the same being is as far beyond the grasp as the idea in theoretical physics that a particle may be in two places at the same time. Perhaps some intuitive understanding of reality is lost to those, like myself, who rely on common sense.

On my second trip to Tibet BK offered the group a trip to Tserpu as an option for a free day. Eager not to miss anything, I was delighted by the opportunity to see another place outside Lhasa. After about twenty miles of paved road we turned onto a dirt track and bumped along through a prosperous valley. On this spring day, the valley teemed with life—people, animals, and renewed seasonal growth. Many small villages sat above the fields that were watered by aquaducts and irrigation ditches. The pastures were littered with stones but also filled with grazing animals: yaks, sheep, goats, horses, burros, cows, and the hybrid cross between cow and yak called *dzo*.

As we pulled into Tserpu's courtyard, BK said, "Crowds come every day. They line up and wait patiently to receive the Karmapa's blessing. If you want to go in to be blessed you need to buy a kathag." Where could we get kathag out here in the countryside? No problem. Near where we parked, some monks were selling the white or yellow polyester scarves for five yuan. We each purchased one and rather irreverently looped them around our necks. Many Tibetans and six or eight tourists wandered randomly in the courtyard before the main hall.

Tserpu is said to have been the richest monastery in Tibet. Today Tserpu reeks of poverty and is painfully plain. During the Cultural Revolution, only the main assembly hall of a large monastery complex was not destroyed. It is a large structure, three stories tall and unadorned. Behind this building some new construction was underway. I have been to Rumtek Monastery in Sikkim which is said to be a reproduction of Tserpu. It's main building is about the same size as at Tserpu but is freshly and exuberantly painted in traditional Tibetan designs. Although not rich by the former standards of Tserpu, Rumtek has a joyous atmosphere.

My impression of gloom at Tserpu was partly inspired by the day which was overcast and chilly. Though it was early June, a snow shower made me grateful for a little bonfire burning in the courtyard. I hovered near it while an extended Tibetan family, including elders and small children, sat on the flagstones picnicking as they waited to see the Karmapa.

The monastery was brimming with animals, dead and alive. In the courtyard a very self-possessed goat seemed thoroughly at home, a few sheep kept their own counsel. At a trough near the kitchen a cow concentrated seriously on eating grain, in a small inner courtyard, we came upon a tethered, tame deer—a very fine, well cared for animal. Along an exterior passageway leading to a few new shrines, several animal heads were displayed like big game hunter's trophies; from the rafters hung a couple of stuffed, much smaller deer and a baby yak. The taxidermy was far from expert and the poor things looked like children's much loved and abused teddy bears—all the worse for wear and neglect.

While I was examining the yak's mangled foot, I heard, "Psst, psst!" Theos caught me by the elbow.

I'm surprised you're here. You didn't write about Tserpu. None of you phantoms did.

"True enough, but I did write about stuffed yaks, remember?"

Oh ... yes. Was that at Gyantse?

"No, Sakya, a dungeon-y room with a herd of dusty, stuffed yaks hanging from the ceiling. When alive the animals carried stones for the construction of the monastery, so keeping their stuffed hides was a way of honoring them for the work they did. They had been put out to pasture and allowed to die a natural death. Very different from trophies in the big game sense."[47]

Inside the main building we went down a side corridor and into a small room full of dreadful masks. "This room was used for Tantric rituals," Theos told me.

"The masks represent the terrors of death," BK added. These masks were truly ugly, though not as gross and gory as the ones boys in the U.S. wear at Halloween. If left alone all night, in this room, a single flickering butter lamp might bring the demon faces terrifyingly alive. Their terrible fangs and multiple staring eyes would be a heart stopping nightmare—an old Tibetan "virtual reality."

"You might explain," Theos said, as we stood in the middle of the dim room, "that I was a student of tantra, not Buddhism per se. Tantric practices exist in Tibetan Buddhism but predated Buddha. My goal in visiting Tibet was to find Tantric manuscripts lost elsewhere."

Let me give your definition of *tantra* then.

> Tantras were the encyclopedias of knowledge of their time, for they dealt with nearly every subject, from the doctrine of the origin of the world to the laws which govern societies, and have always been considered as the repository of esoteric beliefs and practices, particularly those of the Spiritual Science, Yoga, the key to which has always been with the initiate and only passed on by word of mouth. Generically speaking, it is the term for the writings of various traditions which express the whole culture of a certain epoch in the ancient history of India.[48]

About midday the monks directed the pilgrims to form a line. After another wait, the queue to see the Karmapa began creeping forward. We waited until nearly everyone else had entered before taking our place at the end of the line. The audience room was on an upper floor. We climbed the steep ladder-stair, clutching greasy handrails. Just before we entered, two monk bodyguards frisked the men of our group for weapons.

The audience room was not very large. The day's muted light came through two small windows. Only half a dozen people could enter at time, queuing to approach the Karmapa. The room had no decorations, only the throne that reminded me of the story "The Princess and the Pea," for it seemed to be a very high stack of mattresses covered in satin. BK had explained that the Karmapa was an eleven-year-old boy. "He sometimes sits in audience with a bottle of Coca Cola in one hand." The round-faced, slightly pudgy monk sat cross-legged and looked a bit bored—but did not have a Coke when we saw him.

The "audience" drill was simple: one approached, offered the kathag, which was placed in the hands of a monk standing beside the throne, then one bowed one's head to touch a switch of ribbons tied to the end of a four-foot long pole that the Karmapa held—this was the blessing. Before leaving the room another monk put a knotted red loop of yarn over one's head, a gift that had been blessed.

Downstairs again, we glanced into a room off the entryway and saw several young monks sorting and folding the kathag which had been presented earlier and which they would resell the next day to pilgrims—an efficient recycling project, and one of the sources of the monastery's meager income.

"Psst, psst!" Theos was watching the busy monks. "Don't you remember? I wrote that the business monks were the shrewdest—what's the term you use today?"

Wheeler-dealers?

"Yes. The monasteries were rich because they had very astute monks running their affairs."

Recycling the kathag reminds me what you said about the gift eggs.

Theos chuckled. "Oh, yes, the eggs! All a part of the etiquette. One never visited a home in Tibet without both a kathag and a small gift. You know, I wrote that I finally had to find a way to buy kathag wholesale.

> Along with the proper katas very small gifts were given. It is improper to go anywhere in this land empty-handed. The Tibetan usually has a couple dozen eggs on hand, which he passes on at such an occasion, and by the time these eggs have changed hands a couple of hundred times during the several years of friendly intercourse—well, you can imagine what state they are in...If you have a few eggs to start with you are set up for life, as far as visiting is concerned. All who come to you must bring [a gift] too. And you never fail to return a visit.[49]

So, recycling of gifts was a Tibetan custom, very practical.

As we drove back to Lhasa, through the prosperous pasture lands which once had belonged to Tserpu, their springtime abundance contrasted even more sharply with the desolation I had felt at once grand Tserpu. I could not wish for a return to the feudal system wherein the local peasants were serfs, working the land and caring for the animals that all belonged to the monastery, but I cannot tell if life today is better for them or simply just as difficult in a different way.

LHASA TO GYANTSE

BK explained the potential problem at dinner. "There's a big Swiss group going to Gyantse tomorrow, too. The hotel there has promised us the rooms I requested but mostly it's first come, first served. So, if you all don't mind, I'd like to get an early start, say eight o'clock. We'll try to get there first."

When we drove out of the Holiday Inn gate promptly at 8:00, the Swiss group's bus stood in the parking lot with a bustle of activity around it. About twenty-five people were stowing their belongings in the cargo bin. "Ten or fifteen minutes is probably enough," BK muttered. "They won't pass us."

The sun was brilliant, the air pleasantly cool. Autumn couldn't have been more perfect. We traveled through the valley for about an hour. At the Lhasa precinct border we were waved through a police check point— a reminder that travel in this country is not without hassles. We, as dollar-paying tourists, were treated with more deference than others, particularly local Tibetans. Some districts of Tibet are entirely off limits for visitors and several others require special permits.

The paved road ended at an industrialized town in the foothills. We

Yaks, free ranging, beside road and stream

began climbing up the side of the mountain on an unpaved road with no guard rails. Switchback after switchback after switchback. Waddell estimated that the distance, as the crow flies, is about four miles; but it is three or four times that on the ground. We ascended 4,000 feet from the Tsangpo River Valley to Kampa-La. (La is the Tibetan for pass.) Elizabeth's guide book says we would reach 15,724 feet. I was in one of the rear seats of the van where Rinchen Dolma, Theos, and Waddell sat near me.

"We approached Lhasa from Gyantse over this road," Waddell said. "The distance you'll cover today took us over a week."

"A week of staying in some god-awful hovels," Theos groaned.

"My field tent was quite adequate," Waddell commented.

"I tried to warn you, Theos," Rinchen Dolma said.

"Well, there was nothing for it—not being Army or nobility. Anyway, I was so elated to have permission to go to Lhasa, I didn't really mind."

"This was a well-worn trade route. The path was wide enough for two loaded donkeys or yaks to meet," Waddell had adopted his lecturing persona.

"Which is not to say it was a fine, wide road like this," Theos said.

Wide! It's too narrow for my peace of mind.

"This is an example of fine engineering. The track I followed was so precipitous that I did not feel safe on horseback," Theos told me. "I walked most of the way down."

Alexandra had joined the party. "I left Lhasa by this road. I bought a mule and it seemed a pinnacle of luxury to ride up this mountain. Having seen Lhasa, I wouldn't have minded being discovered—although I wasn't."

I believe you were down to under a hundred pounds and not in the best of health.

"That's true, but Lama Yongden shared my privations on the road. We didn't regret a step of the way."

Alexandra, while the van is grinding up this mountain in second gear, and I'm trying not to look over the side, could you distract me with one of your travel incidents? Your reference to the mule reminds of how Yongden took pity on that little donkey.

"Oh, yes. I must explain that Yongden was a lama of the red hat order. The red hats had a reputation throughout Tibet for being masters of divination, which was called *mo*. Quite a bit of our provisions while traveling were gifts from grateful peasants for whom he did mo. So let me tell you this particular incident:

> We met a large party of pilgrims, who certainly numbered more than one hundred, mostly lay people, men and women. Some of them stopped my companion for the inevitable business of casting lots....[One] man had brought with him from his home a small ass which carried his luggage. The object of the mo was to know if it was good, or not, to let the animal go round the Kha Karpo with his owner. If it were foreseen that the journey would turn out badly, the beast would be left at Pedo gompa and the villager would take it home on his way back at the end of his pilgrimage. The little long-eared fellow was not to be consulted, but its good luck had led it to a compassionate friend. Yongden afterward told me that he pictured to himself all the steep climbing that would be hard on the tiny feet of the poor donkey, the high passes, now covered with deep snow, the frosty nights to be passed in the open and all the other troubles which would befall the little slave. How much happier it would be to get a month's rest in the pleasant grazing grounds of the Pedo Valley!
>
> So after appropriate gestures and recitations, the oracle declared that without the least doubt the beast would die if it only came in sight of the Kha Karpo, and that such a death happening during a pilgrimage would greatly diminish the merits and blessed results which each pilgrim expected from

his pious journey! That community of interests was created to insure that not only the master of the animal, but all his companions would look carefully to it that the latter be left behind at Pedo!

Yongden was profusely thanked for his remarkable and most valuable advice, and a few presents entered our provision bags in gratitude.[50]

At last we reach Kampa-la where my phantoms friends met in the opening pages of this book. As Alexandra and Theos noted, Tibetan travelers mark the top of passes with a pile of stones and a mass of laktes, prayer flags on thin poles. "I remember this well," Theos said. "The ridge was marked with the customary collection of streaming prayer-flags, as well as its piles of rock, which grows with the passing of each party bringing another rock to add to the pile for good luck. This was the largest I had yet seen; it was many feet above the head of a man on horseback. As it happened, we arrived at the summit with the pack animals and watched the men one by one adding their gift...[51]

Even as passengers in a van, we shared the joy of reaching this height. We got out to take pictures. A bone chilling wind blew, but the views were too spectacular to miss. Ahead were ramparts of snow covered peaks. Great glaciers hung like ermine stoles carelessly draped on the shoulders of the mountains. I had never been so high. I shivered as I gazed north, down at the valley we had driven through. When I turned to look south, Waddell said, "That's Yomdok Tso, also called Turquoise Lake."

I gasped at the world's highest and, I thought, most beautiful lake. It was unworldly in its calm, for there were no boats of any sort on it, and, from this vantage, I could see no settlements on its shore. Turquoise gems come in many hues and, as clouds passed over portions of the lake changing the light, I saw that it, too, could be many, many varieties of blue and green.

"That's 2,000 feet down," Waddell informed me.

"Give her a few moments to just look and take some pictures. She'll be within sight of the lake for only an hour, but you and I had days to marvel at the color and how it changed," Theos said.

"Well, I took some pains to describe it's geography and I believe that's a bit more useful than trying to describe color in a few inadequate words."

You're probably right, Colonel. Here are your facts:

> The shape of this inland sea was one of the most striking features in the old maps of Tartary. It was figured as a symmetrical ring of water completely enclosing a circle of land in its centre....It's true shape was mapped out for the first time by the Lama surveyor, Ugyen Gyatsho, in 1882-83, who travelled round it and found that the ring was broken in two places, the mountains in the centre forming a bulbous peninsula...When its outline was projected on paper, it had somewhat the shape of a scorpion with recurved tail.[52]

"Of course you can see only a small portion of the whole lake from here. It curves to the left. It's a hundred a fifty miles around, the widest part isn't visible from this road."

BK came over to where several of us were taking photographs. "I see the Swiss bus coming up the road, he said. "Let's not loiter. They'll stop here, too, but I'd like to keep our lead."

As I got back into the van, I heard Alexandra, Theos and Rinchen Dolma call in chorus, "La gayalo. De tamche pham." (The gods win; the demons are defeated.)

As we followed the hair-pinned road down toward the lake, Theos and Waddell began to reminisce about the abundance of fish in the lake.

"There were so many, sometime they were like great moving shadows under the water," Theos said.

"We caught them and they were quite a treat. In fact, a few officers had had the foresight to bring rods and reels. But one didn't need them except for the sport," Waddell said. "Fish were so abundant in this stream below the bridge that they seemed literally to jostle one another, so that some of the Indian followers, wading in, scooped them out onto the bank, and in a short time caught in this way over 300 lbs. weight....Major Iggulden, landed in less than half an hour 48 lbs. weight, many of the fish were lusty fellows scaling 4 to 6 lbs. and giving good play. They were all like carp in general appearance, and almost scaleless...all were excellent eating."[53]

You also noted a lot of wildlife in the area, Colonel, many what you called "Pica hares."

"I saw them, too, by the hundred," Theos added. "The hills are much too windswept and barren to call this area an Eden, but it was a delight to ride through. From time to time we caught sight of geese, ducks and their new goslings and ducklings. Several foxes crossed our trail. Upon seeing us, they would comfortably relax and watch us pass. They did not reveal the slightest fear, a fact sufficiently unusual in my experience of this animal to be worth while to make note of."[54]

Maybe not Eden, but fearless foxes sound like Shangri-la.

As we approached the lake and a town on its shores came into view, I remembered reading that Samding Monastery was near Yomdok Tso. I asked BK if he had never heard of it.

"I know of it but I've been told there's almost nothing left to see," he said. "So I've never stopped."

"Have you heard of the Thunderbolt Sow, a nun—a reincarnation of an important abbess of the nunnery there?"

"No," BK said thoughtfully, "I don't think so."

"But you know what I mean, don't you, Pemba," I asked. "She was the Abbess of Samding, called Dorje Phagmo."

"No," Pemba said. "I've never heard of her."

This surprised me even more than his never having heard of Tsarong Shappé. All my ghost guides wrote of her. I'll quote Rinchen Dolma, as I like to do about Tibetan history.

Dorje Phagmo [Thunderbolt Sow] got her name two and a half centuries ago [in 1716] when the Dzungar Tartars invaded central Tibet, looting villages and monasteries. At the gate of Samding their leader, who had heard that there was treasure hidden in the monastery asked to be let in. The Abbess refused him admission, so he ordered his men to break down the gates. When this had been done the Tartars found the courtyard filled with a large herd of pigs, headed by a huge sow, and the sight disgusted them [because they were Moslems] so much that they turned away immediately. As soon as they were out of sight the pigs again became humans and the huge sow was made Lady Abbess because by her magic powers she had preserved the monastery and its lamas.[55]

"I stopped at Samding," Waddell said. "She was not at the monastery at the time."

"Yes, I wanted to meet her, too but she was away then also. Now, you make we wonder if that was simply the official response to any outsiders," Theos thought aloud. "I'd been told she was one of the most powerful religious figures in Tibet."

"Third in importance after only the Dalai Lama and the Pachen Lama," Waddell said.

I don't like the habit of ranking everything. You two guys keep saying this was the richest, that was the second largest, the third most important in Tibet.

"Dorje Phagmo WAS the most important woman in the religion." Theos reiterated.

"One can't help a bit of ranking," Heinrich added. He was with us, of course. "It was my understanding that only Dalai Lama, the Pachen Lama, and Dorje Phagmo were allowed to ride in sedan chairs."

And I believe you wrote about what happened to her.

150

"When I lived in Lhasa I saw her sometimes. She was a fourteen year old girl, or there about."

Which makes her about the Dalai Lama's age.

"Yes, that would be true. She was a reincarnation, of course. I don't know how many there were since the early eighteenth century. She would come to Lhasa for the festivals. When the Chinese came, she went to India with the first wave of refugees in 1959," Heinrich said. "I wrote about her in *Return to Tibet*.

> ...[she] returned very soon after and allied herself to the Chinese. It is said that by means of her spiritual powers she prevented the drying up of Yamdok Yumtso. She lived in Lhasa, in disregard of her religious vows married...obtained a divorce, had a baby, and permitted herself a rather self-indulgent life. As she was not particularly pretty she must have had some secret powers, as an incarnation, to attract as many men as she was credited with.[56]

Heinrich! What a thing to say! That because she wasn't pretty she should need special powers to attract men.

"Well...?" said all three men in the group.

Really, with all due respect to your ages and times, even so, you must know that a plain woman, by her personality or intellect, often attracts more men than a woman with a pretty face, a svelt figure, and a vapid personality. As for giving up her religion, she may have been coerced. Those who escaped should not be too quick to judge those who endured.

Heinrich nodded agreement, "Yes, we should consider that."

BK told me that on an earlier trip he had seen an aging woman who was dressed like "a mountain woman" (i.e. in a sheepskin chubba). "She was just outside the Jokhang and people were gathered around her asking for blessings. She was certainly someone very powerful." I would like to think he saw Dorje Phagmo, that she is still alive and practices her calling in some way.

After we had gone around the western end of Yomdok Tso and climbed up more mountains, we passed a sizeable village and a little further on stopped in an isolated valley to eat our box lunches. Stones in a field become low stools where we made ourselves comfortable for the highest altitude picnic any of us had ever enjoyed. Although the landscape was desolate, a couple of shepherds appeared. We gave them extra bread and hard boiled eggs. It was uncanny the way a barren landscape was suddenly peopled.

A few miles further on we reached another pass, this one over 17,000 feet high. We parked near where a glacier swept down from the mountain ridge to within a hundred yards of the road. We were busy taking pictures of one another and of the group when the Swiss bus rounded the nearest curve.

"Oh-oh!" As one, we rushed for our van. The big bus stopped beside the glacier and we took off ahead of them again. We hoped that this was their lunch stop—perhaps it was. We didn't see them again until after we had checked into the Gyantse hotel.

Our road ran beside streams with narrow fields in their valleys. Farmers were harvesting wheat and barley using donkeys, yaks, and occasionally small tractors. They cut the grain by hand with scythes and raked it into bundles which were piled in shocks to be loaded on wagons and taken to the village for threshing. In some settlements, most of the houses' flat roofs had become drying racks for hay and straw. These farmers' manual labor brought back very early memories. By the time I turned six my father was able to sell his team of horses and buy a tractor. But I remember walking about through fields of grain tied in shocks like these. The fields in these mountain valleys, some of them terraced, are too small for modern machinery. The only approach is often through the stream and along very narrow lanes. A few Tibetans have small tractors, not much bigger than our riding lawn mowers and these reminded me of my father's first tractor (although it was larger and certainly seemed enormous in my memory). Like these tractors, it had an exhaust pipe in the center of the front, so these farmers, have to breathe the poisonous fumes like my father did.

We sometimes passed large boulders polka dotted with drying dinner plate sized rounds of yak dung, which is a major source of fuel, both for heating and cooking, since trees at this altitude are rare. During my spring time trip, our group noticed, on the road to Yerpa, that a farming village had decorated walls very attractively with rounds of yak dung stacked in standing herringbone patterns. No cord of firewood was ever so artistically arranged.

Now and then we passed a herd of yaks foraging in the fenceless hills. Some grazed roadside while others stood in the middle of the road chewing their cud. Sometimes the van driver had to honk repeatedly before they lumbered away, swishing their tails and shaking their shaggy sides as disgruntled as crockety old men.

"I'll tell you," Heinrich chuckled beside me, "yaks are maddening beasts, but I grew fond of them. Aufschnaiter and I bought five different yaks during the months we were trying to get to Lhasa."

I believe you named them all the same thing.

"Yes. Armin," Heinrich still sounded amused by his memories. "Armin IV we actually bought twice."

I think we've got time for that story. I like it because it shows both the personality of yaks and the difficulty of your travels.

> Late in the afternoon we reached the top of the pass. At last we would be going downhill again. We had finished with wearisome ascents for the time being and glad we were of it. Our yak, however, thought otherwise. He broke away and ran back uphill toward the pass. After endless difficulty we managed to catch him, but we could not get him to move and were obliged to camp in a most inhospitable spot where we could not light a fire...

Next day...we tied a rope round [Armin's] horns and led him over the pass, but he continued to misbehave. We had had enough of Armin IV and determined to exchange him at the next opportunity for another animal.

Our chance came soon. At the next village I made what I thought was a good bargain and exchanged him for a shaky-looking nag. We were overjoyed and went on our way in high spirits.

On the same day we reached a broad valley through which rushed a stream of green water carrying small ice-floes with it. It was the Tsangpo....I found piers of a hanging rope bridge. When we came to it we concluded that the bridge was all right for us to cross but no good for our horse. Animals have to swim, though the coolies manage sometimes to carry their donkeys across the swaying rope bridges on their backs. We tried to drive our horse into the water but he simply would not budge. By this time we were quite accustomed to having trouble with our animals, so I sadly made up my mind to go back to the village and try to effect a re-exchange. It cost me money and hard words to get back Armin, but I got him. He showed no sign of pleasure or of sorrow at seeing me again....

Next morning I forgave Armin all his misdeeds. When we had managed to persuade him to go into the water, he showed himself to be a splendid swimmer. He was often submerged by the rushing water and was carried some way downstream, but that did not disturb him. He swam steadily on, and when he had come to the other side we admired the gallant way in which he breasted the steep bank and shook the water out of his long coat.[57]

Rinchen Dolma was laughing merrily. "You know, we Tibetans were truly blessed to share our country with yaks. I think our people could not have survived in this land with out them."

"Somewhat like the Native Americans and their relationship to the American bison," Theos observed.

Except, Theos, Native Americans never domesticated bison.

"I have a totally unscientific theory," Heinrich said in an uncharacteristically droll tone. "You noticed how patient the workman was when the two little monks teased him. Well, I found Tibetans in general to be patient people and my theory is that they've had to develop that trait in order to live in harmony with their yaks."

"You may be right," Rinchen Dolma laughed. I wrote that yaks were a real gift for Tibet. We used them as both pack and riding animals and they gave the best milk and cheese. (The few without horns were the quietest riding animals and all yaks were wonderfully sure-footed on the roughest and steepest paths.) Their meat was delicious and if properly dried it kept well for a year or more; travellers found it very convenient because when beaten to a powder and flavored with salt and red pepper it could be eaten with tsampa and no other dish was required. Yaks' horns were used to make bottles for water and snuff-boxes which were sometimes ten inches long and looked magnificent when studded with coral, turquoise and amber. Yaks' hooves were eaten, their wool made strong cloth and the best kind of rope, and their ordinary tails were used as dusters while their white tails were valued as fly whisks in India and even went as far as America to make Father Christmas beards.[58]

Yaks' Latin name is *Bos grunniens*, "cow that grunts." They are in the oxen family. Most are black with a white triangular blaze on their foreheads. All have sweeping horns and very shaggy coats, they stand four to five feet tall at the shoulder. Tibetans often decorate their working yaks with tassels of red yarn at their ears—symbols of the cultural and religious, as well as economic value of yaks in this country.

When we reached Gyantse and pulled into the parking area in front of the Chinese run tourist hotel, we immediately saw the hotel mascot, a rare albino yak. He was a beautiful animal with red tassels in his ears. Our whole group remarked sadly that he was not free, but kept in a small pen where he had to breathe the toxic exhaust of buses and vans left idling in the parking lot. We saw him as a symbol of Tibet itself.

GYANTSE

In the room of the Gyantse Hotel that Elizabeth and I shared we found two booklets printed in Chinese and pidgin English. One was a price list that told guests what they would have to pay if they broke, damaged, burned holes in, or appropriated any items belonging to the hotel. The second, a "Notice to Travellers of Staying," contained these directives, among others (typos and misspellings theirs):

> Firearms and ammunition hand over to the local army and police to take care. Setictly forbid criminal offfense as prostitution, visit prostitution, gambling, fight, drug taking spread obscene matter and soon. Be polite to everyone, can't get drunk and create a disturbance, Uproarious and sound loudly to impair another's rest. If you find broken person or a suspicious character, Pease report the Security Department of our hotel and police. If you broken, our hotel have the right to instruct you...if you broken the Criminal Low, you will be investigated the reponsibility for a crime.[59]

Nun at window of nunnery

Through sheer thoughtlessness, or simple lack of aesthetic sense, the hotel rooms looked down on the parking lot and beyond to grain fields. Had it been sited in the opposite direction we could have faced the picturesque Gyantse fort (*dzong*) on its great hill. As it was our view of the fort was from windows in the stairwell. The Holiday Inn in Lhasa, too, could have been sited so many rooms would have had fine views of the Potala—but it wasn't. Chinese builders did not need to consider preferences of guests since this is the official hotel which tour groups are required to use. At the same time, they do not think the town's historic sights sufficiently interesting to take into architectural account. The dzong (or jong, as earlier writers spelled it) was formerly the administrative center of the town and district.

Elizabeth and I made tea with the thermos of boiled water Chinese hotels provide in every room, a touch we agreed would be a nice addition in America. We still had a couple of hours before dinner. "Does anyone want to climb up to the fort with us?" we asked everyone. No one did, so the two of us set off down the dusty, unpaved street.

Theos and Waddell waited beside an alley and beckoned us to come with them. A sign on the wall pointed us toward a steep path. "Kale-kale," Elizabeth chanted our walking mantra.

As usual, Waddell gave a detailed description:

> Passing through a narrow lane of white houses in the Chinese quarter, skirting the south-eastern corner of the rocky hill—which we now saw to be a fine-grained sandstone banded by white quartz, accentuating the boldness of the cliffs—we ascended to the gateway of the fort by a rough stone pavement zigzagging up the face of an almost perpendicular rock, where our path was commanded by a tower on the battlements above. From the ceiling of the portico of the huge gateway—which is about 15 feet high, and supported by massive wooden beams in Tibetan fashion, the

arch being unknown—there hung the stuffed skins of four wild yaks, fearsome with great horns, protruding tongues, and glaring painted eyes.[60]

"Further on we found several tons of gunpowder and about a hundred miles of fuses," Waddell continued.

Yes, Colonel and you certainly couldn't resist using the gunpowder. I saw that you carefully documented in photographs both the gate with several of your Sikh guards and on the next page the cloud of dust when it was blown up.

"Madam, I cannot say I appreciate your sarcastic tone," Waddell said sharply.

About halfway up we entered a small courtyard on the lowest level of fort's compound. We paid a couple of yuan entry fee. A few rooms contained historic displays. One room held a tableau of mannequin Tibetan officials posed as if they were meeting to discuss what to do about the invading British Army in 1904. Another room had a sculpture of Tibetan soldiers in heroic poses with their weapons: slingshots, bows and arrows, axes, spears, and old fashion muzzle-loading rifles. A nearby tablet told the story of the invasion from the Tibetan point of view, listing the generals who led the resistance, some of whom died in battle.

The British force had been just inside the border of Tibet and Sikkim at Yatung and at Chumbi since December 1903 and had taken months to reach Gyantse, having fought several skirmishes on the way. They did not advance to Lhasa from Gyantse for several more weeks. The advance was slow because they needed to build a road for their supply carts and to string a telegraph line. Interestingly the Tibetans never cut this vital communications link although they easily could have at any time. The Tibetans evidently did not know how it worked and had no inkling how desperate the British commanders might have felt if they lost contact with India. Secondly, the Tibetans thought it was an Adriadne's thread, the only way the British would be able to find their way back to India.

At the beginning of this century Britain was the most powerful country in the world but they were bothered by the bully's usual insecurities. They especially feared Russian's imperialistic designs (as Russia progressively annexed various Central Asian countries, almost to the Afghanistan border.) Throughout the last half of the 19th century British adventurers in Asia engaged in what they called The Great Game: diplomatic, military, and spying activities meant to keep India safe from Russian invasion.

At that time, Tibet was the last great nation largely unseen by Western eyes—some twelve million square miles of terra incognita as far as the British were concerned. In his fascinating book *Trespassers On the Roof of the World*, Peter Hopkirk describes the "pundits" who were highly trained Asians, mostly Indians, who traveled in Tibet disguised as pilgrims or traders. They gathered information and made maps. The Great Game players worried about a Mongolian monk named Dorjiev who had ties in the Russian court as well as in Lhasa. They feared Tibet would make an alliance with Russia and tried to negotiate a treaty with the Chinese, stipulating that Tibet would remain neutral or pro-British. But China did not have the authority over Tibet to make such an agreement.

For his 1994 biography of Sir Francis Younghusband, Peter French had access to extensive, recently available documents of the British colonial government. He concluded that:

> Mr. Balfour's Government never wanted to invade Tibet. Rather the advance to Lhasa was the result of manipulation, indecision and chance circumstance, of reaction rather than action...Balfour and his ministers mistrusted the Russophobia of Curzon and Younghusband.[61]

French explains that Indian Viceroy Curzon's popularity was at a nadir with the home government and that Younghusband's career had been stalled for ten years. Each man saw in the other a reflection of his own desire to advance his career by bringing Tibet into the British sphere of control. They cooked up all sorts of excuses for military advance into

Tibet. Eventually Curzon and Younghusband prevailed upon Lord Kitchener, Commander-in-Chief in India. In December 1903, Younghusband was finally promoted to colonel and given permission to go to Gyantse as diplomatic negotiator. To his chagrin, however, Kitchener appointed the ailing Brigadier-General James MacDonald military commander.

Younghusband wrote to the Thirteenth Dalai Lama demanding he sign an agreement that Tibet would not enter into alliances with any other major powers—meaning specifically Russia—but he received no reply. Throughout the episode Tibet's most consistent response to British entreaties and threats was no response at all. Tibetan foreign policy during this whole period was an ostrich-like belief by the Dalai Lama's advisors that by ignoring the entire outside world they would remain invisible behind their mountain bastion. By the time the British reached Gyantse, the Dalai Lama had taken the advice of senior lamas and fled to Mongolia.

Waddell has been pacing about muttering and harumphing during my interpretation of history. "It's very true," Waddell conceded, "that they simply never answered a communication. They never sent envoys with the authority to negotiate an agreement. They only said they wouldn't negotiate at all unless we returned to Sikkim. If the Dalai Lama had come to Yaling we wouldn't have had to mount an expedition at all."

The "expedition" was an impressive assemblage. French describes it thus:

> First came Mounted Infantry, skirting along the edge of the gravelly plain, then the thrusting Colonel and his laggardly General, riding together for form's sake, pursued closely by the dozen men from the Norfolk Regiment with their deadly pair of Maxim Guns: next a handful of British soldiers from the 7th Mountain Battery (armed with two dismanteled ten-pounder screw-guns), followed by nearly a thousand gurkhas and Sikh Pioneers, marching along with their freezing Lee Metford rifles and two elderly seven-pounders known as Bubble and Squeak. Ninety percent of the fighting force was

made up of 'native troops' or sepoys. Under the carefully orchestrated policy of divide and rule, it was a British voice that called the order, an Indian finger that would squeeze the trigger.

Into the distance trailed the army of supporters: the coolie Corps (including several hundred Sikkimese women) with their enormous loads balanced on their shoulders, dodging past the six British military doctors (nicknamed The Troglodytes for their habit of putting up in caves rather than tents), the four newspaper correspondents, anxious for a story, and then the frost-bitten messengers and postal runners, clerks and writers, cooks and bearers, baggage guards and military policemen, the Native Field Hospital Staff, telegraph operators and mess-tent porters, all supported by a trail of bleeding-hoofed bullocks, yaks and mules.[62]

"I call that an invasion!" Alexandra stood before Waddell looking furious and feisty.

"It was an *expedition*. We had no intention of fighting unless we were resisted," Waddell said between clenched teeth.

"You entered a neutral country," Alexandra challenged.

"Madam—"

"Really, Waddell," Theos, too, joined the fray. "You've got to admit your entry into Tibet looked like, walked like, and quacked like an invasion. You can't wonder that the Tibetans called it an invasion."

I pointed to the statue.

There are the weapons the Tibetans had to use against your modern guns. The few battles the Tibetans waged against you were unequal to put it mildly.

"Yes, that's true. The poor wretches all carried amulets blessed by the Dalai Lama which they thought would protect them against harm. Don't forget we dressed the wounded on the battle fields—those who would stay put and let us help them. They were quite surprised and grateful."

"Don't break your arm patting yourself on the back, Colonel," Theos said. "I can think of no moral excuse for killing the Tibetans."

"Self-defense," Waddell snapped. "We suffered losses, too, you know."

Mostly Gurkhas, about whose deaths you were rather cavalier in your book.

Alexandra added, "The tablet says they fought well."

"Of course it says that. They wrote it." Waddell stalked out of the room in frustration.

"I say, Waddell," Theos called after him in a mock British accent, "Did you really sleep in caves?"

"Military matters curdle my blood." Alexandra shivered as she spoke. "But the view from here is spectacular."

"Come with me, I'll point out where our estate was," Rinchen Dolma said, taking Alexandra's hand.

"I'll come too," Theos chimed in. "I truly enjoyed visiting you and Jigme there. Those afternoons were very stimulating. You were both so invested in helping make Tibet a modern country."

All of us climbed higher up. As Waddell's description went on to note, the fort is a series of buildings on higher and higher levels, reached by a switchbacked path. The buildings were shut, the whole place felt neglected. Finally we climbed a ladder to the dizzying height of the topmost roof. I caught my breath and imagined Younghusband, his balding head shining and bushy soup-strainer moustache blowing in the breeze as he stood here with the Union Jack flying above his head. He would have lifted binoculars to eyes and scanned the valley to the south where supplies would arrive, and then looked the opposite direction for messengers or troops from Lhasa. He also would have watched with suspicion the comings and goings of the monks down below in the monastery since he believed, often correctly, that the lamas were plotting resistance.

The monastery, Palchor Chode, tomorrow's destination, was embraced by a stony mountain arm. A natural stone ridge stretched from behind the monastery to the fort and had been partially blown up by the British.

From our bird's eye vantage, I saw that the town was entirely sur-rounded by fields of grain that were being harvested. The landscape was gold, the distant mountains turned pastel in the late afternoon light. A rain shower passed far up the valley but didn't threaten us. Standing on the highest point for many miles around made me euphoric. Elizabeth agreed she would enjoy watching the sunset from here, but we had been told to be at the hotel for dinner at 6:30.

Although Gyantse is Tibet's third largest city, it had no sidewalks and didn't seem to need them. Two-wheeled carts drawn by donkeys and puttering little trucks and tractors are the most common traffic in the streets. The only reminder that this was the end of the 20th century was a couple of big modern tractors with enclosed cabs which probably belong to collective farms here in this broad valley where they could be used effectively in large, flat fields.

A farmer drove a herd of yaks and dzos right down the main street like a scene from Dodge City. A Khampa rode by on his pony, a rifle slung across his back. He wore traditional brown wool robes, his black hair wrapped with a hank of bright red yarn. Marlboro Man, Tibetan style.

After-dinner entertainment consisted of a pool table in the hotel lobby. Someone suggested, "Let's go out and look at the stars." Gyantse had almost no street lights and nothing obstructed our view. Even the dzong and its hill shrunk to insignificance under the expanse of sky. I had often read that the thinness of the air makes the stars shine more brilliantly here than elsewhere. The stars above us were brilliant and stunningly multitudinous. We wandered about the parking lot hugging ourselves against the evening chill, our heads thrown back as we gazed at the sky, bumping into each other as if we were drunk on stardust.

We heard first one bark, then an answer, then several howls from dif-ferent directions. Elizabeth's guidebook said that dogs take over the town of Gyantse after ten o'clock, prowl all night, and then sleep all day. We looked toward the street a little apprehensively and noticed a closed gate at the entrance to the parking lot. Near the gate a guard stood smok-ing. Was he protecting us or keeping us in? We hadn't taken seriously the information that there is a ten o'clock curfew in Gyantse. BK told us that sometimes the Chinese military move through the city at night and they don't want us foreigners counting trucks or troops, or to know if they are carrying nuclear waste to a dumping site in the mountains.

On May 24th, 1937, Theos Bernard arrived in Gyantse. According to the Tibetan calendar, the following day was, as he wrote, "Dawa Shi nyam chu naga, the fifteenth day of the fourth month, the most auspicious day of the year, for it marked the enlightenment and the ascension of the Lord Buddha into Nirvana."[63]

"Whether it was pure accident, the working of fate, or an instance of unexplained synchronicity, it was the single most fortuitous event of my life," Theos said.

"Theos," Alexandra said rather sternly, "Why are you suddenly diffident. Don't you agree with me that chance is but an easy word to describe unknown causes."

"I do agree with you," Theos said, sounding more sure of himself. "When the abbot learned that I had come to study Buddhism, wanted to read sacred texts in their language, had practiced physical and mental yoga disciplines intensely, and that I was trying to learn spoken Tibetan, he believed my arrival was fated. He welcomed me and made me part of ceremonies which no Westerner had ever seen."

"Remarkable," Alexandra agreed. "No wonder, as you said, they thought you might be a reincarnation. Perhaps you were."

Really, Alexandra, are you serious?

"Tibet has magic and mysteries most Westerners find difficult to comprehend," Alexandra told me.

"Thank you, Madam David-Neel. I thought you didn't like me," Theos said, flirting a little—a natural response to any woman who seems interested in him.

Some men are like that, which Alexandra, the ex-opera singer, understood quite well. "I've met a good many reincarnated lamas who were difficult human beings...and others who were wise, saintly even, and some with very mixed personalities. A man is a man after all," she said.

When we arrived at the monastery, we found that the Swiss group had preempted us. "They're a typical tour group, they'll rush through and be out in fifteen minutes," BK said. "Let's wait a bit."

Theos stood surveying the monastery. "I sound like a stuck phonograph record, I suppose but, this is not the monastery I saw in 1936. I see only half a dozen buildings, it was a small city—well, a town. Fifteen hundred monks lived here."

As Theos is telling me this, BK is saying the same thing and adding, "Now about fifty live here."

Waddell wrote:

> The monastery is peculiar in being of a catholic kind, tenated by both yellow- and red-cap sects....These diverse sects thus housed together live side by side as in different colleges within one wall. Each has its own separate cluster of temples and residential buildings, dormitories, store-rooms, etc., where each lives according to its own customs and rites, not mixing with the others except at "High Mass" in the general assembly hall...The great temple or "house of the gods" is Egyptian in its massiveness and in the tapering style of its walls. Its three-storeyed facade, a fine specimen of wooden architecture, [is] brilliant in crimson and green and gold.[64]

Theos had made a circuit of the courtyard that was empty except for a collection of dogs, all mutts, every size, shape and color. "Fifty-nine years ago, at dawn, this courtyard was my first glimpse of the splendor and pomp that I would discover in all the great monasteries of Tibet. When we arrived in the early morning, all the monks were seated on long hand-woven carpets in the large courtyard in front of the main building....The higher Lamas formed two parallel lines in the center of the great gathering, while the head Lama sat on a high chair at the end farthest removed from the entrance, through which we were led to the private room of the Abbot.[65]

The main "temple," as Waddell called it, is not as splendidly painted as in his day. But beside it the elaborate chorten called the Kumbum, which literally means 100,000 Buddhas, was resplendent with a new coat of shiny white paint and oriental scroll designs in turquoise and gold. The structure is 107 feet tall and has 108 doors, the vast majority of which lead to small shrines. Waddell says the Kumbum was built as a replica of "the great pagoda of Gaya in India erected on the hub of the Buddhist universe, the spot where the sage Sakya obtained his supreme enlightenment and became a Buddha." He goes on to give an architecturally informed description of this remarkable building:

> This pagoda is nearly 100 feet high, with a circumference at its base of about 2000 yards, and has the eternal form of a chorten which is considered to symbolize the five elements into which bodies are resolved on death [earth, water, fire, air, ether]...It has stepped terraces of plinths below, surmounted by a drum-shaped body which is crowned by the spire of a great gilt ring and an umbrella canopy. It is eight storeys high, the lower five forming the steps of the plinth, the sixth the great drum and the seventh the gilt spire and its basement. Each of these terraced storeys has an outer balustrade, reached by an inner stair, for the pilgrims to perambulate around and enter the shrines on each flat. It may be considered an octagonal building with the alternate faces notched into a double recess, an arrangement that gives a many-cornered star shape of twelve faces to each storey, and a vertical ribbing to the sides of the building. In each of the twelve faces is a small chapel dedicated to a different Buddhist divinity....Entrance is gained to the upper storeys by inside stairs, which go off to the right and left of the central chapel facing the entrance.[66]

168

We climbed up level by level and explored several shrines, not as a group, but by ones and twos at our own pace. I grew bored. The shrines were small and dim, full of wall paintings and statues. The 100,000 Buddhas could provide material for a doctoral thesis on their subtle variations.

I stopped ducking through the usually low (five foot high) doorways. The bright sun was quickly warming the day. On such autumn mornings when the shade is chilly, standing in the sun is pure sensual pleasure—even more so when it is under an intensely blue sky surrounded by the diamond-pure light of Tibet. While others studied the shrines, I found sunny corners in the sun and looked up to the dzong silhouetted on its towering hill and out over the courtyard. Below a party of five barefoot Tibetan pilgrim women in traditional dark dresses and striped aprons were circumambulating inside the monastery wall, prostrating at each step.

Pemba had learned that a prayer service would soon take place in the assembly hall. In the meantime we explored the upper level with its special shrines. A locked altar room which contained a wonderful ancient mandala was opened for us. Other designs around the room including pictures of sexual union (*yab-yum*) revealed that this was a Tantric chapel. Butter lamps burned at the shrine, as always, but the room felt dusty and little-used. I wondered if anyone alive in Tibet could help a young student understand the complex meanings of this room's symbolic images.

In the dark, chilly assembly hall a handful of monks took their places and the chanting began. Members of our group spread out, took seats around the perimeter of the hall or stood at the back wall. I was approaching chanting overload. After about fifteen minutes I went out, seeking the warm sunshine.

Theos met me at the doorway with a reproachful look. "What's your problem today?"

It's dark and cold in there, and beautiful out here, I've had enough chanting for a while.

"You've only been here a week; I was here three months. Haven't you realized that each monastery has its own personality and each is a different experience."

Yes, but boredom is a valid experience, too.

"Granted. Now the monasteries are bleak and depressing."

It was spring when you arrived, would you say that the ceremony celebrating Buddha's enlightenment is somewhat analogous to Easter?

"No, I really wouldn't say that," Theos snapped. "Why is it necessary to liken other cultures to our own? Waddell wrote about 'high mass.' Buddhism isn't Roman Catholicism."

Well, comparative religion...

"Can be a drag. It obscures uniqueness. Making analogies is a way for small minds to stuff new experiences into little pigeonholes instead of expanding and appreciating the variousness of different cultures."

The ceremony you saw here seems to have taken you by surprise.

"That ceremony was the beginning of an emotional and spiritual journey that was more powerful than I could have imagined. I tried to say how it affected me."

> There were three thousand candles in the dimly lighted sanctuary, in your wildest imagination [you] will never be able to picture the impressiveness of these hundreds of twinkling lights which were placed in a row of two completely around the room....The Buddha was of the most impressive size, all studded with precious stones. The sixteen Buddhasatvas which are usually painted on the walls were represented here in giant figures adding immensely to the impressiveness of the environment which would instill religious devotion in any soul—even the most hardened heathen would want to bow or do something. That is the

feeling it gives you, that you must do something, you know not what and you know not why, but something deep within is moved that perhaps you never realized existed before.[67]

Then three days later you saw the brief display of the great thanka.

"Two-thirds of the great thanka. The Abbot told me one third was carried off by the British to one of their museums. The rest was displayed on the wall behind the monastery. I got up well before dawn, hoping to photograph the hanging of it, but it was too dark. However, the sun was rising when it had been hung so I used my telephoto lens. I climbed around on the roofs of the buildings and got the picture that's in my book. The thanka was only displayed for an hour, and then rolled up again before the sun could fade its colors."

Heinrich was standing in the shade of the portico listening to us. "I saw the great thanka at the Potala being hung. I'm not a religious man, but anyone was bound to feel he was witnessing something extraordinary."

"Well," Theos gave me a reproachful look, "our writer here is bored and needs a respite."

Yes, I do, guys, sorry.

As they moved away, they continued talking about photography. I heard Heinrich say, "When I tried to take pictures of the procession of the Dalai Lama from the Potala to Norbulinka, even though I had his permission, many ordinary people were angry. I was nearly attacked."

"Believe me I know about how angry they could get. I was actually stoned once when I was photographing at Chakpori Hill," Theos said.

They went toward the Kumbum leaving me on the steps of the assembly hall near a pair of young monks. One cleaned and polished small butter lamps. He knocked lumps of fatty residue out and threw them to the dogs who gulped them down. The other monk tore off bits of cotton from a roll and twisted them into wicks for candles. They worked slowly and deliberately. These were chores, a menial and boring part of life, necessary but certainly not onerous.

Being in the countryside, even though it's literally on the other side of the world, inspired memories of my rural childhood. I recalled summer afternoons when I would sit on the concrete steps of our porch with a dishpan full of shelling beans in my lap and work in the sun. I day dreamed, only peripherally aware of birds twittering in the cedar trees, or our gabbling pet geese as they wandered around the yard searching the grass for bugs. I worked with neither enthusiasm or resentment, doing a chore that simply needed to be done. I have no idea what these young men's lives are like, what their concerns and hopes are, but I feel I have known the languid mental quiet that comes from doing a simple chore in the sun.

After lunch we visited a nunnery which was built on the other side of the wall of rock surrounding the monastery. As we crossed a small footbridge below the nunnery, Waddell walked beside me. "In 1905 there were three nunneries in Gyantse. The nuns were quite a sight, all shaven headed. Some wore ordinary monk's conical yellow caps, but a few had huge fluffy wigs of curly wool, giving the appearance of the great frizzy, shaggy shock-head of a South Sea Islander. These nuns were very plain in looks, dirty and illiterate. They go begging about the town and villages....Only one could write. Their few books were all manuals of worship and charms for sacrificial rites.[68]

We found the nuns much more attractive than did Waddell. In fact some of them were charming and all were young. Their hair was shorn to the scalp; not a wig was in sight. They shared poverty with their predecessors, but these nuns did not beg, they worked in the fields.

BK had made friends with a sweet, diminutive, hunchbacked nun. She was young, no more than thirty. I saw him greet her in the Jokhang on our first day in Lhasa and heard him promise we would visit her and he would bring photographs. In Gyantse she welcomed him like an old friend with her extremely pretty, though shy, smile and she was delighted with the photographs.

On a previous visit the nuns had held a special prayer ceremony for BK's group and had promised to do so again any time he returned. However we were told that most of the nuns were in the fields harvesting potatoes and they couldn't stop for a prayer ceremony. But BK implored, persevered, and cajoled, so eventually someone was sent to the fields to call them in.

While we waited we visited an elderly monk who lived in an enclosed cave which he had not left for seventeen years. He had been praying continuously for the Dalai Lama's return. Just outside the monk's cave geraniums bloomed in pots and water boiled in a teakettle heated by a parabolic reflector cooker such as we saw in nearly all the monasteries. Two concave aluminum shields, adjusted to the angle of the sun, re-flected the sun's rays at the kettle which was perched on a stand. Water was boiling, we heard it, saw the steam from the spout.

"That's an interesting and useful device," Alexandra said, coming out of a nearby building. "They're making herbal medicines in there and need a lot of hot water."

In a country that is fuel poor but has plenty of sunshine, even simple solar energy devices like this make very good sense.

"I was thinking how useful when people love to drink tea as much as Tibetans do," Alexandra said.

We visited a new, unfinished assembly hall and walked among the low buildings that looked like a 1950s motel. A series of doors opened into small rooms which were the nun's cells. The buildings are sparely deco-rated with flowers in window boxes and peach-colored plaster swirled in decorative patterns on the exterior walls. The whole nunnery feels new, revealing that, to some extent, a return to the religious life is tak-ing place.

New York Times writer Seymour Topping, who visited Tibet in 1979 with his photographer wife, Audrey, wrote an introduction to Audrey's picture book in which he quotes dreadful statistics: 120,000 monks lived in Tibet in 1950 and only 2,000 were alive and practicing in 1979. This explains the lack of older monks and nuns today. Those not killed were forced out of their monasteries into secular life, and, says Topping, some 30,000 fled the country in the wake of the Dalai Lama's exodus.

After a while the nuns arrived from the potato fields. Their little, ticky-tack assembly hall was by far the most modest we saw but the new one would be finished soon. The nuns sat in two rows and pulled their cloaks around their shoulders. Some took up three-foot-long horns and some played drums. All chanted.

Although earlier in the day I was tired of listening to rituals, the higher pitched women's voices gave the chanting an ethereal quality. They punctuated their prayers with bursts of horn blowing and drum banging. I was overcome by a sense of ugly-American-ism, feeling ashamed that since we could pay we would get what we wanted, even interrupting their work in the fields in order to hear them "perform." Then I told myself maybe we gave them a welcome respite. Most people digging potatoes welcome a break to sit down and sing.

Back at the hotel Elizabeth suggested we go out into the barley and wheat fields to take photographs of peasants at work. We stopped to watch a family of prosperous farmers. The husband had a tractor and a small wagon which was piled high with straw held in place with ropes. When he pulled up to a patch of mown ground his wife quickly helped him untie the ropes and then the farmer pulled the lever that lifted the wagon bed so the straw was dumped in a pile. A child who had been waiting with her mother solemnly watched her parents work.

I remembered being such a child fifty years ago, at the end of the Second World War, when rural Southern Indiana was just beginning to mechanize. In my very early memory my father and his brothers mowed wheat fields with a scythe as some Tibetans are doing today. Horses pulled the wagons and plows. These fields are barley and coarse legumes for animals, not the wheat of the American Midwest, but I recalled the sweet scent of newly harvested grain. After threshing, our wheat was stored in a big bin in the barn which was much better than a sand pile to play in. I could sift it through my fingers, half bury myself in it, and even eat some of the ripe, nutty grains.

I also remembered riding on top of a wagon load of hay. It seemed huge and high and was pulled by a team of sturdy farm horses which were larger than Tibetan ponies. I felt like King of the Mountain riding from the field to the barnyard up there with my Uncle Jim while my father rode on the tongue of the wagon holding the horses' reins.

In the wheat field I met a young woman raking mown grain with two men—brothers? Husbands? (For polyandry and polygamy were, and still are, a part of the Tibetan social structure.)

She said, "Hello."

"Hello," I answered

"Where are you from?"

"America."

"America good." The young woman had exhausted her English vocabulary but she took my hand and turned it over. She stroked the palm several times after which she held my fingers, running them across her palm, showing me it was rough and calloused. She took a hand of one of the young men and displayed his even more calloused palm. He smiled and made raking motions, inferring that is why their hands are not soft like mine. I nodded and mimicked to show my understanding. If I had the words I would tell them my mother and father worked like they are working and shared their callouses.

The woman pointed to my camera asking me to take her picture. Then, noticing Elizabeth approaching, she signaled that she wanted Elizabeth to take the picture of us together. Elizabeth obliged. The woman held my hand lingeringly when I said good-bye. At home I studied her features in the picture and didn't know if she was Tibetan or Chinese—whichever, she was a hard worker who pointed out, matter of factly, that a gap separates us. Whatever I wished I could tell her about understanding farm work, it is obvious that I have been able to leave the farm which she is unlikely to do.

175

"Do you think these people are Tibetan or Chinese?" Elizabeth asked as we were leaving the fields.

"I think Tibetan, but these could be collective farms, so I guess they might be Chinese," I said.

"I wonder who lives in that tent." Elizabeth nodded toward a black felt tent at the edge of the field.

"Tibetans," I answered.

A little boy of about three came hurtling out of the tent and threw himself violently at Elizabeth's knees. He was ragged and filthy, his hair stuck out in all directions so uncombed it was almost in dreadlocks. Elizabeth was briefly shocked by being nearly knocked over, but she found candy in her pockets and gave him some. A dog beside the tent began to bark. The child's mother, also dirty and unkempt, came out of the tent, and an even smaller, filthy faced child peered from behind the tent flap. Elizabeth gave them all treats and asked if she could take their picture. Before she got her camera ready, a third child appeared, a school-boy of seven or eight, thin but washed, wearing a neat cap and jacket. He had a solemn, serious look.

Returning to the hotel Elizabeth said, "He really tackled me. It wasn't a game, he wanted to hurt me." Alexandra and Theos both wrote about the xenophobia of rural Tibetans. Foreigners were sometimes stoned. Alexandra was constantly concerned about being recognized as a for-eigner fearing for her physical safety as well as being turned over to authorities and deported. Elizabeth's attacker was only a child, perhaps assuming the role the masstifs play at farm houses: defending against intrusion, a very basic instinct.

We wondered if the family lived in a tent all the time, if there was a father who worked in the fields. They were the poorest, dirtiest people we had seen so far. The older boy may be the only literate one in the family but, presumably the other children will go to school. Surely edu-cation is a positive good, they may have a better life than their parents.

Is "better life" a reflexive formula, meaning nothing more than acquiring materials "goods"?

Alexandra David-Neel, in pilgrim's robes and lama hat

SHALU

On the way to Shigatse, we turned off the main road and followed a track for three or four miles, crossing a dry stream bed, and navigating around boulders. Gyantse valley was wide and fertile, watered by a river that ran through it but this area was high desert with no ripening grain fields. We passed a line of crumbling adobe pylons that had been telephone poles. Trees were unavailable when telephone lines were strung but now the Chinese have trucked in poles so the pylons are no longer used.

Our destination was Shalu, a small monastery that looked very ancient. In fact it was founded in 1027. In the monastery courtyard a few gnarled trees somehow kept a tenuous hold on life, their leaves limp and gray with dust. A few dusty dogs lay sleeping in the shade. BK and Pemba went to find some monks to let them know we were there and to see if any ceremonies were about to take place.

Theos and Alexandra came toward me from the group of buildings to the right of the courtyard.

I didn't think either of you came here.

"I stopped here in 1916 when I visited Tashilungpo," Alexandra said.

"No, I didn't see Shalu," Theos affirmed, "It's small and out of the way and I couldn't get to all the interesting monasteries in a short trip. This is one I wish I could have visited, though. I had read mention of it in Alexandra's book. You should know that Shalu was once a retreat destination especially for monks doing long periods of meditation, very often three years, three months, three weeks, three days, three hours."

To gain enlightenment?

"Tradition has it that they studied what you'd call magic." Theos said.

"Didn't BK tell you that about Shalu?" Alexandra asked. "As you know, one of my books was renamed when it was republished in the 1960's, *Magic and Mystery in Tibet*. I wrote about several adepts who had studied here."

"You recounted all sorts of amazing things in that book—"

"You're intrigued. Admit it! Everyone is," Theos teased. "I certainly found it fascinating."

I'm fascinated but skeptical.

"Powers that seem supernormal are a matter of physical discipline, of changing the body functions through mental control and breathing exercises," Alexandra said. "That's why accomplishments that seem supernatural can be taught."

You both might be surprised that the "magic" practice I've heard most about I read of first in a book by the movie star, Shirley McLaine. She reports making herself warm by visualizing a sun in her solar plexus. Not long after that I read somewhere about a traveler who saw monks in the Himalayas walking barefoot in the snow wearing only light cotton robes. The snow falling on them melted as if it fell on a hot stove.

"You're talking about *tumo*," Alexandra said. "I wrote very specifically about the method of learning it. In this terrain it's an extremely useful accomplishment."

Theos added, "Milarepa, the 11th century poet and Buddhist saint, was called 'the cotton clad one' because he only wore light robes. He stayed warm by practicing tumo."

I have no difficulty believing people can learn to raise their peripheral temperature. Other things are more far fetched.

"Such as?" Alexandra asked.

For instance, you write that you created a *tulpa*—a kind of psychic extension.

"Psychic extension! I never used those words."

Okay, before I get into more hot water with you, Alexandra, I'll quote your American biographers, Michael and Barbara Foster who told the tulpa incident succinctly:

> Alexandra intended to manufacture an entity that hadn't existed previously, a lama, "short and fat, of an innocent and jolly type..." [she wrote] "After a few months the phantom monk was formed. His form grew gradually fixed and life-like looking. He became a kind of guest, living in my apartment. I then broke my seclusion and started for a tour."
>
> The monk tagged along, walking by her when she rode and stopping as they made camp. Sometimes the illusion rubbed against her, palpably touching her. Worse, "the features... gradually underwent a change. The fat, chubby-cheeked fellow grew leaner, his face assumed a vaguely mocking, sly, malignant look. He became more troublesome and bold. In brief, he escaped my control."
>
> ...With her usual determination Alexandra forcibly decided to dissolve the phantom. But the mind-creature clung tenaciously to life, and he only disappeared after six months of hard struggle, presumably after she had performed the appropriate meditations.[69]

"That was an unfortunate incident, and it cost me a great deal of effort, but it was a vivid lesson. When you have not only seen but felt such a being—and others also saw him—dissolving him is extremely difficult."

I understand hallucinations and self-hypnosis but... "Oh, DO you?" Theos challenged.

"You know she doesn't," Alexandra said, talking past me, not to me.

So what did people learn here at Shalu?

"Shalu's special reputation, when I traveled and studied in Tibet, was for teaching the *lung-gom-pa* technique."

Yes, you wrote about three sighting. The first gives us a picture of what a lung-gom-pa does.

> Toward the end of the afternoon...riding across a wide tableland...I noticed, far away in front of us, a moving black spot which my field-glasses showed to be a man. I felt astonished. Meetings are not frequent in that region, for the last ten days we had not seen a human being.
>
> ...By the time he had nearly reached us; I could clearly see his perfectly calm impassive face and wide-open eyes with their gaze fixed on some invisible far-distant object situated somewhere high up in space. The man did not run. He seemed to lift himself from the ground, proceeded by leaps. It looked as if he had been endowed with the elasticity of a ball and rebounded each time his feet touched the ground. His steps had the regularity of a pendulum...
>
> My servants dismounted and bowed their heads to the ground as the lama passed before us, but he went on his way apparently unaware of our presence.[70]

"My second experience was quite different," Alexandra continued.

> We were travelling in a forest, Yongden and I walked ahead of our servants and beasts, when at the turning of the path, we came upon a naked man with iron chains rolled all round his body. He was seated on a rock and seemed so deeply buried in thoughts that he had not heard us coming.

We stopped, astonished, but he must have suddenly become aware of our presence, for after gazing at us a moment, he jumped up and threw himself into the thickets more quickly than a deer. For a while we heard the noise of the chains jingling on his body growing rapidly fainter and fainter, then all was silence again.

'That man was a lung-gom-pa,' said Yongden to me. 'I have already seen one like him. They wear these chains to make themselves heavy, for through the practice of lung-gom, their bodies have become so light that they are always in danger of floating in the air.'[71]

"Fascinating," Theos said. "I saw an oracle float. I had barely crossed the border from Sikkim; I was at Tung Kara Gompa in the Chumbi valley. It was our good fortune to arrive at the monastery when their oracle was about to go into one of his trances. We witnessed the entire performance from the time he entered the separate shrine, where the spirit is supposed to dwell, amid the chants and clashing of cymbals which are said to prepare him for his trance. The spirit in him then started talking at a frantic speed and writers tried to take down every word as he floated about the room. When he collapsed from exhaustion several of the attendants caught him in their arms lowering him to the throne without bodily injury.[72]

"Yes, yes," Alexandra said impatiently. "Such things are not unusual. You interrupted me."

"I found it unusual, most Westerners would," Theos said testily. "I thought this was a conversation, not a lecture."

"I wanted to go on to my third example which connects us to Shalu. I was traveling in Kham, in Eastern Tibet with a small caravan. We met a poor pilgrim carrying his luggage on his back as Yongden and I did a couple of years later. Back then thousands of such people were on the tracks all over Tibet and solitary travelers had a habit of attaching themselves to caravans. The traveler said he had been staying at Pabong

Monastery in Kham and was on his way to the province of Tsang—
which is where we are now. It was a long journey, but not unusual in
those days. He was with us for several days and we thought little about
him. But one day we had some troubles and didn't get started until late,
so Yongden and I went ahead of the rest of the group with only one servant who was carrying provisions for tea and our dinner. We stopped at
a grassy spot near a brooklet, well ahead of the rest of the caravan, and
had already had tea when I saw the pilgrim climbing the slope toward
us progressing with extraordinary rapidity and when he got nearer I
could see his gait was that of a lung-gom-pa.

When he reached us, the man stood quite still for a while staring
straight before him. He was not at all out of breath, but appeared only
half conscious and incapable of speaking or moving. However the trance
gradually subsided...Answering my questions, he told me that he had
begun the lung-gom training for acquiring fleetness with a gompchen
who lived near the Pabong monastery. His master having left the country,
he intended to go to Shalu gompa...He confessed to Yongden that the
trance had come on him involuntarily and had been produced by a most
vulgar thought. As he was walking along the servants...were going so
slowly he thought we were no doubt grilling on the fire the meat he had
seen my servant carrying with him...he visualized...the fire, the meat on
the red embers, and sunk in contemplation gradually became unconscious of his surroundings. Then prompted by the desire of sharing our
meal, he accelerated his pace and in doing so mechanically fell into the
special gait which he was learning....The third day after his racing performance, when we awoke, at daybreak, he was no longer in the tents.
He had fled at night, perhaps using his power of lung-gom and, this
time, for a more worthy purpose than that of sharing a `bonne bouche.'[73]

"It was a different world, back then," Alexandra said. Everything is in
ruins now. The most important teachings were never written down.
Today's monks and nuns have no one to teach them the difficult, esoteric
practices. They can only learn Buddhism from the books. I'm glad I was
here when I was. I was able to study many of the Bon practices also."

I'm glad your *Magic and Mystery in Tibet* can still be found.

"I only hope people will read it as seriously as I meant it. I was accused of writing for shock value. I was always a serious scholar," Alexandra said. "Please tell people that."

You just did.

Visiting a monastery where lamas are supposed to have learned magic is provocative. This modest, dusty place was listed in BK's book as a "power place," which is why he sought it out.

BK appeared with a gaggle of young monks. We slowly circumambulated Shalu's assembly hall looking at the faded murals on the walls, which were difficult to see in the scant light from small clerestory windows. Even in the light of a strong flashlight they were dimmed by hundreds of years of residue from butter lamps. From there we went to more private shrines on the upper level. A monk took the padlock off the door to a very old shrine room which was the artistic highlight of Tibet for me. The walls were covered with mandalas in softly aged colors, two on each wall, each about eight by eight feet, each different. Mandalas are complex maps of the world as the Buddhists understand it—three planes: physical, psychic-spiritual and "astral." Robert Fisher, in *Art of Tibet*, wrote that Shalu and Drathang monasteries have the best preserved early art still extant in Tibet. At Shalu, paintings are the work of a Nepalese artist, Anige, and his artisan-assistants, begun after 1306. Fisher does not specifically write about these mandalas, so I am not sure they are Anige's work, and perhaps they aren't quite that old, but they are stunning examples of a very high artistic tradition and well deserve to be kept behind locked doors.

Below the mandalas was a row of busts of lamas who had lived here. They all wore yellow robes and pointed yellow hats. At first they seemed alike, but if one looked closely they became individual. Studying their faces I wondered, what did they accomplish? What practices for overcoming laws of nature did they learn? Or did they?

The point of a devotee's meditation is not to gain paranormal powers. Buddhists believe such powers do nothing to free the soul from samsara and suffering, although their attainment may be a marker of progress. If the possessor of special powers uses them for his own ends—whether financial or to control others—they become destructive to the user, a black magic roadblock on the path to enlightenment.

The monk who had let us in opened a special compartment near the Buddha statue and took out a small scroll wrapped in red silk. He explained it was written by a lama who was the abbot of Shalu; he did not say how long ago. The monk blessed us by tapping us on the forehead with the scroll. In this windowless space, I shined my flashlight over the masterpiece mandala maps of the worlds and into the staring eyes of the lama statues. I was reluctant to leave this wonderful room; the young monk became impatient to close the door so I moved on.

Another very old shrine, opposite the mandala room, would have fascinated Theos. BK said it was the most special, but, for me, its fanged, many-eyed angry deities and coupling divinities were horrible and frantic after the orderly serenity of the mandalas. The two shrines seemed two poles, like the Dionesian and Apollonian philosophies of Greece; one physical, the other intellectual. Even as these thoughts came to me, I saw Theos wagging a finger, reminding me that the Eastern practices do not necessarily fit Western models.

I paused on a balcony outside these private shrines and tried to communicate with a few monks who were fascinated by my watch and flashlight. I thought of Alexandra and the pilgrim with unsuspected abilities; none of these young men had a mystical look. The teachers are gone but...who knows?

Rinchen Dolma climbed up from the courtyard carrying a copy of her book, *Daughter of Tibet*. "I wrote that we Tibetans, as Buddhists, ought not be superstitious, but most of us are. We know that spirits exist and many of us experienced remarkable things. Do you remember the spirit the Abbot of Sakya gave my mother? I was only a child but the whole household shared my fear."

Rinchen Dolma, I think others will feel as bewildered as I am about this example of Tibetan "magic." But, as the one Tibetan ghost guide, what you wrote has special interest for me.

> [The Sakya Lama] suggested she [my mother] should take care of one of the *dumo* (she demons) of Sakya, who would then be her escort on her many journeys. So she took care of Hrikyila and was given a small mask of this dumo and instructions on how to feed her by burning tsampa and herbs. The Sakya Lama considered that my mother had enough religious power to control Hrikyila. There were many dumo at Sakya in a special temple—sometimes they are called *khandoma*, which means 'angel' and is a more polite way of referring to them. They were souls of women who had died in anger and had gone to Sakya, as only the Sakya Lama could control them; under this guidance some of them gradually became enlightened and purified...they were strictly confined by order of the Sakya Lama; but sometimes they were disobedient and went to Lhasa or other places and he was requested to call them back. They became a bit frightening when they were not under discipline.[74]

Our group of middle-aged seekers was, of course, conversant with superstitions, psychic phenomena, various kinds of divinations, and new age–ish beliefs. Early on Felicity confided that she uses the Tarot to focus on both personal and professional problems. Later in the trip, by divining with a crystal used as a pendulum, Denise helped Pat decide which souvenirs she would give to each of her children. When Denise and I were roommates in Kathmandu we discussed subjects like automatic writing and ghosts both of which she had experienced. I have experienced neither but admit I regularly throw coins for *I Ching* readings; I find deep wisdom in that ancient book.

Once, the world was quieter and those with a talent for introspection and observation became shaman, priests, and yogis. They dedicated themselves to disciplined accomplishments which were passed from teacher to disciple during lengthy periods of study. We know that drugs, fasting, physical exertion, sensory deprivation, and breath control are among the things that produce altered psychic states. The ancient yogis and lamas learned to use these elements to specific ends. In this era's spirit of looking for physiological explanations for what we do not understand, I would add the suggestion that Tibet's thinner air may cause body and brain chemistry to work a little differently than it does nearer sea level.

Some writers, like Waddell, filled their books about Tibet with facts and measurements, discussions of geography and wildlife. Some, like Younghusband, eventually fell into a romantic mysticism, and others who never travelled to Tibet, like James Hilton, author of *Lost Horizon*, captured the public's attention with romantic tall tales. But several Westerners like Theos and Alexandra came to Tibet as active, informed seekers of psychic "literacy." Alexandra's erudition was taken seriously by Sidkeong Tulku, the British educated prince of Sikkim who was also a recognized reincarnated teacher. He invited her to lecture at monasteries and gave her the title *jetsuma*, "learned lady." I've been told that Theos' Ph.D. thesis, *Hatha Yogi*, remains a respected text. When they returned from Tibet both gave lectures and then retreated to study and contemplate the texts they had gathered.

In 1967, at age ninety-six, Alexandra wrote a new introduction when *Magic and Mystery in Tibet* was republished in England. She said:

> ...seekers after miracles would perhaps be most surprised to hear me say that Tibetans don't believe in miracles, that is to say, in supernatural happenings. They consider the extraordinary facts which astonish us to be the work of natural energies which come into action in exceptional circumstances, or through the skill of someone who knows how to

release them, or sometimes, though the agency of an individual who unknowingly contains within himself the elements apt to move certain material or mental mechanisms which produce extraordinary phenomena.

...I did not go to Tibet with the idea of seeing miracles there....in the course of my travels I witnessed unusual events, met strange people and brushed the threshold of a particular spirituality.[75]

Perhaps because Shalu is small, rural and dusty, the paintings have survived while fabulously wealthy monasteries like Tserpu were destroyed. When I looked at the statues of the lamas who had lived and taught here, I thought those men were literate in a psychic dimension the West does not understand. In the rarely visited shrine rooms, I felt the memory of magic, if not magic itself.

Tiger from painting on entry gate

SHIGATSE AND TASHILUNGPO

Shigatse is the second largest city in Tibet. Parts of it are westernized but it had the feel of many small cities I knew in Indiana. The buildings were low, only three or four stories—a city that does not need elevators. The streets were wide with a little truck traffic, several people on bicycles, a few donkey carts. Shigatse had a quiet, sleepy look, a feeling of dustiness and distance, at least in the eyes of a New Yorker. To rural Tibetans it is probably a bustling, and maybe even intimidating place. Signs over shops were in Chinese and/or Tibetan script and sometimes English. Not far from the big Chinese-run hotel we passed the Petroleum Restaurant. "Ah-ha, the local greasy spoon!" I laughed.

"Oil exploration was a big thing around here for a while," BK said. "It must have seemed like an inviting name for a restaurant."

"That's not where we're having dinner, is it?"

"No, no, no."

Our first destination was a rug factory. Young women, plump and apple cheeked, worked at big, upright looms threading wool through warp threads, then hammering it tightly against the preceding threads. The pounding made quite a racket. I pitied any young woman who might have come to work with a headache. They paused to smile at us, talking softly to one another about their visitors. Pemba explained to them, I think, who we were. The second room was devoted to sculpting. Men plied electric clippers along designs, producing a dimensional surface and filling the air with lint. In a sales gallery rug after rug was laid out, traditional and modern designs, rich color combinations, large and small rugs. They were a bargain, but only Pat purchased one. Outside, in a grassy courtyard, a couple of young women watched and played with several toddlers—day care for the children of the rug weavers.

When we boarded the van again BK said, "We can go back to the hotel and relax, or we can go to a market for an hour while the driver gets gas for the van. There's only one gas station, and the negotiations are so complex I prefer to leave it in his hands." We opted for the market. Situated along a broad street, the open air market had cloth awnings to shade the simple displays laid out on platforms a couple of feet up from the pavement. Behind the street was a steep hill on top of which were ruins of the dzong of the Tsang province of which Shigatse is the capital. The building is entirely gone, only jagged remnants of the foundation remain.

Theos was standing near the market staring at the hill. "Unbelievable," he muttered. "Just unbelievable. I feel I had a vivid dream, then I woke up and—" He snapped his fingers, "everything disappeared."

Yes, a vast fortress has totally disappeared. You didn't make a special point to describe it, as Waddell might have, but what you said in your diary gives an impression:

> It was a steep ride to the top entrance to the jong so we had to take it rather slow. Once we had arrived and led the horses thru its winding passes to the official stable, we had to climb as much as tho we were visiting the Potala. The Jongpen's servants were waiting to receive us and it was but a moment before we were in his presence....He has a well lighted small room at the top of this high fortress which dates back before the founding of the Potala."[76]

"I was as shocked as you are," Heinrich said as he, too, gazed dolefully at the jagged profile of the rocks above the marketplace. He sighed. "Well, instead of dwelling once again on all that's gone, I'll mention that the market is livelier now than in '82. As I said:

> Shigatse too was a scene of ruin and devastation, with nothing remaining of one of Tibet's finest fortresses; no prayer-flags and no mani walls, those walls engraved with prayer formulas. The colourful and one-time lively square below the castle was derelict....Here, in the past, sat the peasant women with their head ornaments arranged in a big hoop, consisting, according to their means, of precious pearls, turquoise and coral. These arched head ornaments distinguished them from the Lhasa women, whose ornaments were arranged as triangles...A few peasant women were still sitting on the ground, offering their wares, but there were no ornaments on their heads.[77]

Heinrich, I'm afraid the magnificent headdresses have vanished everywhere.

"The women would have made peacocks envious," Theos said.

Yes, the various jeweled constructions were unlike anything I've seen in pictures of other cultures. They must have been uncomfortable to wear but I wish I could have seen them.

Most of the venders we saw were young women in modern slacks and tops. They were extremely aggressive in trying to sell their cheap jewelry and trinkets insisting everything was "cheap, cheap" and all "very old Tibeti silver."

I found an iron Buddha hand, torn from a statue; I bargained and bought it. Now it lies on my coffee table. I wonder to which monastery it once belonged and what stories of violence and destruction it has been through.

The bazaar also sold useful items like dishpans, mutton and acrylic yarn but nothing was quite as fascinating as the dentist Heinrich mentioned seeing in 1982:

> The biggest attraction in the bazaar, however, was a dentist who treated his patients with an ancient treadle-drill, surrounded by curious onlookers. The patients did not suffer from bad teeth but merely from vanity. I watched the 'dental surgeon' file a groove into a tooth and fit some facings of gleaming metal into it. These facings—cheap but glittering like gold—were laid out on a little table for customers to choose, and next to them lay a hammer and a pair of pliers.[78]

Dinner was at a Chinese cafe a few doors from the Petroleum Restaurant. Except for the Lhasa Holiday Inn with its European chef, food in the official Chinese hotels is terrible. In Gyantse BK and YD somehow got permission to use the hotel kitchen where YD prepared spaghetti and tomato sauce which they had brought from Kathmandu, along with a container of Kraft parmesean cheese. At breakfast the next morning we were grateful when YD appeared with some left over spaghetti—an indication of just how bad the breakfast buffet was. The only thing the hotel cooks were unable to render dry and tasteless was boiled eggs.

Elizabeth and I shared one of the few rooms decorated Tibetan style, complete with thick carpets on the benches that were later made up as beds, traditional designs painted on wall and ceiling, and a large shrine. The treat for our eyes was equaled by the delight of a huge old fashioned bathtub and plenty of hot water. However, we were glad Elizabeth had brought candles since the electricity went off about 8:00 and didn't come back on. The next morning, after breakfast, as I went down the hotel's pretentiously grand staircase with its inferior carpeting over poured concrete, Theos, looking tall and scruffily bearded, and Alexandra, small and now in early twentieth century clothing, were waiting.

Alexandra, everyone will know you're not a pilgrim.

"When I was here in Shigatse in 1916 I didn't have to disguise myself. I traveled with a few bearers and donkeys and stayed in the private home of the sister of the Tashi Lama while I studied with a geshe."

Theos and Alexandra got into the van with me. Theos said, "I promise, even if you're getting tired of monasteries, you'll find Tashilungpo unforgettable."

Tashilungpo Monastery is the seat of the head of the red hat sect, the Panchen Lama. (Older books, such as Alexandra's, called him the Tashi Lama). The Dalai Lama is the head of the yellow hat sect and is the incarnation of Chenresig, the patron deity of Tibet. The Panchen Lama is an incarnation of an equally important aspect of Buddha. Although traditionally a rivalry exists between Lhasa and Shigatse, which has been played on by the Chinese for hundreds of years, the two high lamas have a religious and political bond.

In a 1996 article in *Vanity Fair* Alex Schoumatoff wrote:

> "... it was the Fifth Dalai Lama who created the Panchen Lama lineage in the 17th century...In the Tibetan panoply of 'living Buddhas,' the Dalai Lama and the Panchen Lama are the sun and moon, the queen and the rook, whichever of them outlives the other leads the search for the deceased's reincarnation..." [79]

At present the Dalai Lama and the Tibetan government-in-exile have recognized a boy as the reincarnation of the Panchen Lama. The Chinese authorities have chosen a different boy whose education they are overseeing. The whereabouts of the boy selected by the Dalai Lama is not known. There are rumors that the Chinese have imprisoned him and his parents. Other rumors say he has been taken to India. Chinese politics are now, as they have always been, extremely complex. Tibetan reincarnation theology is equally complex. The Dalai Lama is quoted by Schoumatoff as explaining:

"...two separate emanations from the same source can coexist. There are several kinds of reincarnation: One, the previous self takes a new body. Two, the ultimate source of the reincarnation can multiply simultaneously, so in that case rebirth may not necessarily come after a previous death. Two reincarnations can happen, for instance, there are two of the Taklun Tsetul, one in central Tibet, the other in eastern."[80]

We parked just outside a gateway on which wonderfully animated, almost psychedelic, tigers and snow lions had been recently painted. Once inside the gate, we had entered a large village that looked the way Tibet's monasteries must have in the past. Buildings were separated from one another by cobbled walks and alleys, occasionally leaving space for a patch of hollyhocks, a few silvery-green willows, or a sunny nook where several lazy dogs dozed. On a hill overlooking the monastery, and visible from far away, was the thanka structure that looked like a concrete screen for a drive-in movie. It seemed to be waiting for a time when sound and light shows will project pageants of carefully packaged Sinocized Tibetan history on the screen while recorded chants boom from a speaker system.

Tashilungpo was relatively safe from Chinese destruction because the Panchen Lamas have, for many generations, had particularly strong ties with China. The 10th Panchen Lama, who died in 1989, did not go into exile like the Dalai Lama and so many others. He is sometimes called a quisling for cooperating with the Communists but, in fact, his story is far more complicated.

The Panchen Lama was only three years younger than the Dalai Lama and they probably became friends in their teens. The Panchen Lama was forced by the Chinese to marry (there is one child from that marriage; widow and child live in Beijing), and he was subjected to a fifty-day public trial during which he was spat on, punched, and humiliated; but he never repudiated the Dalai Lama's position. He was then imprisoned for ten years (some reports say fourteen). When he finally returned to Tashilungpo and was allowed to speak in public he affirmed that the Dalai Lama is the rightful ruler of Tibet. This sparked an anti-Chinese riot that was brutally suppressed and the Panchen Lama was never allowed to give another public speech.

After restrictions were relaxed in the early '80s, the Panchen Lama was allowed to live at Tashilungpo, but at age fifty he died suddenly of a "heart attack." He was overweight and fit the "at risk for coronary disease profile," but many Tibetan and Western political writers believe he was poisoned. (Poisoning has traditionally been the disposal method of choice for troublesome high lamas. Several Dalai Lamas between the Sixth and the Thirteenth died before they were able to take over the government from their regents—by poisoning, it is believed.)

In any case, the Tibetans never questioned the Panchen Lama's holiness. They had placed his picture beside that of the Dalai Lama in most of the shrines we saw. On my return trip, even though the Dalai Lama's pictures had been removed, the Panchen Lama's pictures were allowed to remain.

As an American, I learned about separation of church and state as if it were a self-evident truth without which no citizenry could live freely or happily. But when I read the history of Tibet, I found no instance when the theocratic rulers outlawed the Bon religion and read that Moslems and people of other faiths lived and worked freely in Tibet, including Italian Capuchin missionaries who built a church in Lhasa and resided there from 1707 to 1745.

Chinese attempts to impose Communist ideology in place of religion has clearly failed so they are trying to mold future religious leaders—the Karmapa and the Panchen Lama—by choosing boys to train and install instead of those chosen by the Tibetan government-in-exile. Tibetan logic is not the rigid either-or of Western thought and at various periods of their history, Tibet has paid allegiance to China while pursuing their own way of life. It seems to me that if Tibet were truly an "autonomous region"—as the Chinese claim it is and the heavy handed rule of Chinese officals prove it is not—peaceful coexistence would be possible as the Dalai Lama has repeatedly affirmed.

As we walked across the broad courtyard, Theos said, "I attended a sunrise ceremony here in this courtyard, very much like the one at Gyantse."

I know, so I won't quote that description, but I will share with the others what you said about the wealth of Tashilungpo.

> When I was at Gyantse I spoke with exaggerated emotions of the religious wealth which glittered before my eyes at the end of those long dark passages thru which we were led with a small butter lamp. When at Lhasa, I reached another all time high when trying to reveal the grandeur of the late Dalai Lama's tomb. Now if you will put all of this together and multiply it an infinite number of times your imagination will just commence to ascend the threshold of my present experience...virtually all of [the statues] were gold plated and many in pure gold....It was a matter of passing from shrine to shrine in rapid succession. Each shrine was about fifty feet in length and filled from the floor to the ceiling with small images which were the fierce representation of the chief life size deity in the center along with all of his disciples.[81]

As Theos did, we explored the maze that is Tashilungpo Monastery and, on an upper level, we walked through a series of shrine rooms that contained hundreds of small statues arranged on shelves—as in a treasure house—which it is. The gold seems to have disappeared; most of the figures we saw were silver. They were examples of the master silversmiths, exquisitely molded, bejeweled, displaying enormously imaginative variety. These rooms also held silk embroidered thankas and beautiful, old silk brocade hangings and canopies. Each room had one or two monk guardians. In one room the young guardian sat in a small window seat, a book on his lap, napping...until we entered when he quickly sat up straight and looked official.

Tashilungpo is the only monastery at which we saw a group of elderly monks. The Gyuto monks who chanted at Ramoche were mostly middle-aged and at Drepung and Sera we saw a few middle-aged men, but the majority of monks were quite young. Here, in an upper level room, deep within the monastery, fifteen or twenty wisened old monks sat at tables where they wrote out prayers for pilgrims, for a price. One old monk near the doorway was especially conscientious and demanding about the fee for photographing in the room. As these old men dealt with their "clients" they were querulous, bad tempered, anything but serene. They were all very bent, wrinkled, balding, and nearly toothless.

I walked with Pat to a balcony that overlooked a courtyard. "I didn't like those monks," she said.

"Neither did I," I agreed.

Alexandra and Rinchen Dolma came along the balcony to join me as Pat went on to explore other areas. Rinchen Dolma said to me gently, "You should remember these men lived through the entire recent history of Tibet. Very likely they suffered a great deal, probably prison and torture. When they were boys learning by rote like the little ones you saw at Drepung, or as older students debating scripture no one was preparing himself to face the destruction of his way of life."

"Yes," Alexandra added. "Try to imagine what reservoirs of strength and character were depleted just to endure."

I can't imagine it, Alexandra. I have the impression from Alan Watts and other writers of the '60s that Buddhists are laid back, peaceful, serene, transcendent, beyond the pettinesses the rest of us know so much about.

"Ridiculous," Alexandra snapped. "I, for one, never became what you would call 'laid back.' So what of people imprisoned for their beliefs, who have lived through famine and forced labor?"

Theos came around the balcony to join us. "You know, I wrote in my diary that the majority of monks were anything but holy people. They had chosen an easy life and were as petty, quarrelsome, lazy, insolent, and self-serving as people in any other field—like many lower-level workers in any large corporation."

In your diaries you, too, are short tempered and intolerant with distressing regularity.

"I did have a short fuse; but my fits of pique blew over as quickly as a summer thunderstorm. I did everything intensely." He gave me a wink, "That's why you like me so much."

Yes, I admit it. Also, you didn't sleep enough when you were in Tibet, you tried to do everything as fast as possible, photograph everything and meet everybody.

"It was high adventure, I loved it! An incredible journey. I didn't want to waste a minute of my short stay."

"He didn't tolerate fools gladly. And neither did I," Alexandra added. "We came looking for the best of Tibet. We had to take the bad that came with it but we didn't have to like it."

"Alexandra's right, we came to learn." Theos said. "Right here, in those shrines, I found most of the guardian monks didn't even know what the statues represented, I corrected them quite a few times. A visitor was lucky indeed if he was invited into the hidden rooms to meet the erudite lamas."

"Yes, the few, not the many," Alexandra said. "I found that to be true in every monastery I visited. But I will say, I thoroughly enjoyed living here those several weeks."

My real life companions were wandering about in ones and twos. I was afraid I would get lost in this vast monastery if I did not follow them.

In an alley, I met some country women in traditional costumes. One even wore a sheepskin chubba such as mountain people all wore fifty years ago. These women had huge pieces of amber and turquoise in their hair and wore jeweled amulet boxes at their waists. However, the children with them had been dressed in modern shirts—all of them red and festive.

On the middle level I followed the sound of chanting; I knew that

200

would have attracted BK and Mark. I found them in an unusually arranged assembly hall. Unlike most such places, the major shrine was not
directly ahead of the entrance behind a statue of Buddha, but was off to
one side of the room. Also I could not circumambulate the room because benches crowded with monks lined the walls. Above them the
ceiling was equally crowded with hanging thankas. This assembly hall
reverberated with a different kind of music. Monks of many ages
chanted individually, not in unison. Their voices created a contrapuntal
music without a dominant motif. Listening to this chanting was more
fascinating, and in a strange way, even more uplifting than any other
chanting I had heard. The room, chock-full of monks, young and old,
made me think of many people practicing Bach, each playing a different
fugue, some on organs, some on harpsichords. Within the chaos was a
clear form for each individual.

"The rooms were always packed like this," Theos said. "I didn't care
for these individual sessions, but when a ceremony was going on, with
the drums, cymbals, horns and conch shells punctuating the chants, the
place aglow with butter lamps, it did something to the old insides.
You're lifted out of yourself."

"Mass hysteria." I turned and saw Heinrich standing at my side. "All
of us who lived through the Nazi era—" he coughs and doesn't finish the
sentence.

"Or trained to be soldiers," said Waddell. I did not expect either of
them here, but they are the voices of my own skepticism.

"Individuality is often very tenuous." Alexandra opined.

Isn't the point of your meditations, Theos and Alexandra, to slough off
your individuality and become one with some ALL? And, isn't that what
happens when we sing in unison—hymns or mantras—when we dance
or when, as Waddell would agree, soldiers go into battle, perhaps even
when assembly line workers get into the rhythm of their jobs or, as
Heinrich suggested, when we are caught up in a mob. The self slips away
from us when listening to music or watching theatre, even watching a

movie. Maybe that's why Americans today are addicted to action films and theme parks.

"Enough! Enough!" Theos laughed. "Save it until you get home. You've got amazing sights to see here yet."

When I left the assembly hall I joined several of our group sitting on a wide stone stairway that descended to the courtyard. Waiting for others to join us, we relaxed in the sun and watched a few dogs wander about, noses to the ground, sniffing for food or the scent of their friends. From inside the hall, we heard a jubilant cry. Suddenly monks, rushed out. Like a river released when the locks of a dam are opened, a cascade of maroon robes billowed and blew past us, they rushed down the steps, across the courtyard and away. Within a minute or two the courtyard was again quiet and almost empty.

Good heavens!

Alexandra sat beside me laughing. "They're hungry. It's lunch time."

Besides the huge thanka structure, Tashilungpo monastery includes two other amazingly large constructions. One is the largest statue of Buddha in Tibet. The Buddha Maitreya is nearly 90 feet tall—about nine stories high. It is gilded with over ten thousand ounces of gold and embellished with turquoise, coral, amber, and other jewels. Standing before the enormous Buddha, one's head falls back as one's gaze goes past the golden hands that rest in a meditative position on vast knees, up to the golden chest and up over the nicely shaped chin to the broad, squarish face which has an almost smiling mouth, a straight nose, and very long, but slightly closed eyes. One's eyes travel on up to the thin, shapely eyebrows and the jewel between the brows in the forehead, and up, and up over the forehead to the large, jeweled, lotus-shaped crown. Light from the high clerestory windows illuminated the head, the only other light comes from butter lamps on the altar.

The stupid, overused word, "wow" involuntarily escaped my half-opened mouth.

Many pilgrims and worshipers filed in, walked around the statue, added butter to the lamps, prostrated, and prayed. In a dark corner the guardian monks sat chanting softly. No, I thought, bigger is not better or more beautiful. This Buddha had a comprehensible face—serenity I could understand—but the colossal size tinged it with self-importance, ostentation. I did not like this statue, it took up too much space. One could not breathe in such an overwhelmed atmosphere.

"Tell them the story of the dedication of this giant Buddha Meitreya," Alexandra said.

When was that, Alexandra?

"In 1917, not long after I left Tashilungpo. When I was here I heard a great deal about Kyongbu Rinpoche but I did not meet him because he was very elderly and in permanent retreat. He was the 9th Tashi Lama's spiritual advisor. A very holy man. The Tashi Lama was very proud of this giant Maitreya."

> The Tashi Lama wished his old spiritual advisor to perform the consecration rite, but the latter declined, saying that he would have passed away before the temple could be finished. To this the Tashi Lama replied, beseeching the hermit to delay his death till he had blessed the new building....
>
> The hermit promised to perform the consecration. Then, the temple being ready and a day appointed...the Tashi Lama sent a beautiful sedan-chair and an escort to Kyongbu Rinpoche to bring him to Tashilungpo's gompa. The men of the escort saw the lama sitting in the chair. The latter was closed and the porters started.
>
> Now thousands of people had gathered at Tashilungpo for the religious festival of inauguration. To their utmost astonishment they saw the lama coming alone and on foot. Silently he crossed the temple threshold, walked straight towards the giant image of Maitreya until his body touched it, and then gradually became incorporated with it. Some

time later the sedan-chair with the escort arrived. Attendants opened it's door...the chair was empty.[82]

When you wrote about it you offered four possible explanations, all of which are as incredible as the story itself since they involve a body double or a ghost.

"No normal explanation was possible," Alexandra said. "The rinpoche's physical body was never seen again."

"I've heard stories like that," Theos said. "Now come, there is a physical body you must see."

We went to see the enormous shrine that is the tomb of the 10th Panchen Lama. A recent *New York Times* article by Seth Faison, who was writing about the two Panchen reincarnations, said that in life the Panchen Lama was a large man who had a commanding voice that "could range from the deepest rumble to a high-pitched squeal in a single sentence." His pictures that I saw in shrines everywhere gave me the impression of an avuncular man, though that seems a decidedly mistaken idea.

The tomb itself was a seven-layered structure, a chorten, gilded gold and studded with gems. Since it was quite new, the thousand Buddhas painted on the walls of the room that enclosed it were vivid, the fabrics in the many hangings were brocaded silks in a rainbow of primary colors. Everything was shiny, bright, and opulent. At the top of the chorten was a throne, a shell-shaped structure with a wide gold frame. Seated inside the frame in the lotus position was the mummified and gilded body of the 10th Panchen Lama. Not a statue, mind you, the REAL body. All the features of the face were clearly defined in a gold mask with carmine lips and heavy ebony eyebrows. His right hand was raised and he held a bell in two fingers with a delicately raised pinkie. He was clothed in a yellow silk garment, draped over his shoulders was a beautiful brocade robe, lined in red.

The whole spectacle, as it was meant to be, was stunning. If there is one thing at which this century excels it is building stupendously tasteless, bigger than necessary structures. But the colossal isn't a new idea. Many of the ancient sites I have long been fascinated by were on a grand scale, of which the grandest were in ancient Egypt. The gold faced Panchen Lama, of course, recalled Tutankamen's—more beautiful—gold funerary mask.

During an earlier trip to Egypt, my guide, a trained archeologist, often explained how the ancient Egyptian priests planned the temples so that light fell from above in shafts. The sunlight illuminated particularly stunning paintings and statues. At the end of a long, dark corridor, in the holiest of holies, the golden statue of the god stood behind closed doors. The priests used incense, chanting, musical instruments and the drama of drawing open a series of doors to make the golden idol appear awe-inspiringly, brilliantly aglow at the climax of a ceremony.

Several times my guide explained, "That's how the priests made the people's hearts to quiver." He pointed out that the priests exploited the people by keeping them illiterate, indebted to the religious establishment and heavily taxed. The men were conscripted, forced to labor part of the year, building the ever greater temples, royal palaces, and tombs. This guide's description of ancient Egypt was very much like the description of pre-Communist Tibet given by the Chinese to Audrey Topping in 1979 when she was among the first Western visitors since the 1950 take-over. She dutifully repeated the official version in her book.

This gold faced Panchen Lama on his shining throne was an example of how the priests of Tibet "made the people's hearts to quiver." The new chorten is grander, shinier, than even the Great Fifth's tomb in the Potala, which in it's time served the same purpose.

Out in the sunshine once more, I walked through the cobbled alleys between pastel stuccoed buildings. Alexandra and Theos walked on either side, nodding sympathetically at my mixed feelings now that I had seen the one monastery in Tibet that most retained the pre-1959 atmosphere. I had not seen it all—not by a long shot—but after that giant Buddha, the gilded Panchen Lama, the chanting, the flash flood of monks

I was both impressed and depressed. I had another set of vivid images to add to those from all the other monasteries, from little Gonggar to mysterious Shalu.

We had lunch and began the four-hour drive to Lhasa along the Tsangpo, our last look at Tibetan countryside. Both Theos and Heinrich have noted that the same route between Shigatse and Lhasa used to take four or five days on horseback. My journey in Tibet was ending. I wished I lived in that slower paced era so that for a few days I could simply be in this mountain-gird desert-like country at the top of the world, following the upper reaches of one of the great rivers of Asia. I needed to mull over and integrated what I had seen and experienced.

We reached Lhasa and had a free hour before dinner. Some of the group wanted to go to the Jokhang and Barkor for meditation and shopping. I asked to be dropped off in front of the Potala. I paused for some time in front of that historic building: grand, empty, enormously evocative. The thin, clear air gave every detail the sharp unreality and clarity of a recurrent dream image. The afternoon sun was piercingly bright, the sky was that Tibetan blue, the color of eternity. The twelve hundred room palace had a majestic simplicity and elegance that does not hint at the baroque profusion of images in its hundreds of rooms. Just a few glints of the golden roofs were visible from where I stood on the expanse of concrete that was a water meadow in old photographs.

A small Tibetan woman, perhaps twenty-five years old, paused beside me. She pointed to the palace. "Dalai Lama," she said then she clasped her hands before her face and bowed her head. I did the same and she looked into my eyes and smiled then went on her way. Our meeting was only a minute but I felt sure she wanted me to know that the Potala is the rightful home of the Dalai Lama and that she wishes for his return and she smiled because she knew I felt the same.

EPILOGUE

Theos, Heinrich, and Rinchen Dolma all wrote about the Tibetan custom of riding several miles out of the city either to meet arriving guests or to accompany them on their departure. On the morning we were leaving Tibet, we got up very early—again in order to get started before the Swiss group, since airplane reservations are no more binding than hotel reservations. In the dark we set out for the sixty-mile drive to Gonggar airport and all my phantom guides piled in around me for part of the trip.

"I wrote many more books," Alexandra said. "You should try to find those that have been translated into English. And if you're ever in the south of France, stop at my home which is now a museum at Digne."

I would like to do both, Alexandra.

"I too wrote more," Waddell said. "I wrote quite a study of lamaism."

I do know that, Colonel. I believe it's somewhat dated now. But don't look so angry, I was lucky to have come across your book by chance. You gave me a good account of the invasion.

"Mission!"

If you must call it that. I also appreciated the precision of your information, especially architectural.

"Well," said Heinrich, "you've seen both my books and you have my book of photographs."

That's right, and I've even see the movie—

"Please, the less said the better."

I agree, Heinrich. Your before-and-after books were an inspiration for what I've tried to write. And, dear Rinchen Dolma, I knew of you before I found your book. I had seen beguiling pictures of you and your husband in Theos' book.

"Speaking of—" Theos said. "Are you saving the best for last?" He winked at me.

I would say that only because you are my special discovery. I feel only one degree removed from you.

"I'm not sure I understand."

A well-known drama called *Six Degrees of Separation* suggested that everyone is no more than six steps removed from everyone else on the planet. In respect to you, my friends, I include the no longer living in that theory. Through your ex-wife, Theos, I am only one degree removed from you. And through you, I am only two degrees removed from Rinchen Dolma. Through Rinchen Dolma I am only three degrees removed from Heinrich and through Heinrich, four degrees removed from the Dalai Lama.

"If you're going to go on in that vein," said Alexandra, "You are not so far removed from me either, for Theos tells me he studied with my teacher the Lachen Gompchen. Thus..."

Quite right, Alexandra.

"I have no idea, Madam, how you could claim any acquaintance with me," said Waddell.

"Ah, Colonel, it's really very simple. I happen to know that Theos met Younghusband, so there's the connection."

"Well, I find it all very far fetched," Waddell said.

208

"Not at all, Waddell," Heinrich corrected. "In the web of life, we are all connected."

That was my point, but, in fact, I feel connected to all of you in a closer way, for I have read and reread your words; I have had an intellectual dialogue with each of you. I only hope that my words will send others to your books and to other books and perhaps inspire some to visit Tibet. Most of all, I hope readers will care about this beautiful country, it's beleaguered culture, and it's people—both in Tibet and in exile.

The sun was rising, the sky was turning gold above the mountains. As ghosts do, my phantom guides faded away; but they remain very alive in their books and in my mind.

I have quoted a great deal and will end with a quote, the last line of Theos' unpublished journal. He had been up all night, pecking away in his two-fingered method at the Smith Corona typewriter he took to Tibet. He wrote "...so with the dawn I close the daily account of a dream."

BIBLIOGRAPHY

Bass, Catriona, *Inside the Treasure House: A Time in Tibet*, Victor Gollancz Ltd., London, 1990.

Bernard, Theos, *Penthouse of the Gods*, Scribners, New York, 1938.

———, *Hatha Yoga*, Rider and Company, London, 1950.

———, Unpublished letter and diaries of travels in Tibet.

David-Neel, Alexandra, *My Journey to Lhasa*, Times Books International, New Delhi, 1991 (Original edition: 1927).

———, *Magic and Mystery in Tibet*, Mandala Books, Unwin Paperbacks, London 1984 (original edition: 1967).

Foster, Barbara and Michael, *Forbidden Journey, The Life of Alexandra David-Neel*, Harper & Row, San Francisco, 1987.

Fisher, Robert E., *Art of Tibet*, Thames and Hudson, London, 1997.

French, Patrick, *Younghusband, The Last Great Imperial Adventurer*, Flamingo, imprint of HarperCollins, London, 1994.

Harrer, Heinrich, *Seven Years in Tibet*, Paladin Grafton Books, London, 1988 (original edition: 1953).

———, *Return to Tibet*, Penguin Books, London, 1983.

———, *Lost Lhasa: Heinrich Harrer's Tibet*, Harry N. Abrams, New York, 1997.

Hopkirk, Peter, *Tresspassers on the Roof of the World*, Jeremy T. Tarcher, Inc., Los Angeles, 1982.

Johnson, Sandy, *The Book of Tibetan Elders*, Riverhead Books, New York, 1996.

Kristoff, Nicholas D. and Wudunn, Sheryl, *China Wakes, The Struggle for the Soul of a Rising Power*, Vintage Books, New York, 1995.

Schoumatoff, Alex, "Sun Without a Moon," *Vanity Fair*, New York, NY, August, 1996.

Taring, Rinchen Dolma, *Daughter of Tibet, The Autobiography of Rinchen Rinchen Dolma Taring*, Wisdom Tibet Book, John Murray, London, 1970.

Topping, Audrey, *Splendors of Tibet*, Sino Publications, New York, 1980.

Tung, Rosemary Jones, *A Portrait of Lost Tibet*, University of California Press, Berkeley and Los Angeles, CA, 1980.

Waddell, L. Austine, *Lhasa and Its Mysteries*, Dover Publications, New York, 1988, (original edition: London, 1905).

Tibet, Jugoslovenska Revija, Belgrade & Shanghai People's Art Publishing House, 1981.

END NOTES

1. Bernard, Unpublished dairy, entry May 19, 1937
2. Waddell, *Lhasa and Its Mysteries*, p. 339
3. Harrer, *Seven Years In Tibet*, p. 170
4. Bernard, *Penthouse of the Gods*, pp. 145–6
5. Ibid., pp. 152-3
6. Waddell, *Lhasa and Its Mysteries*, pp. 362–3
7. Taring, *Daughter of Tibet*, pp. 79–80
8. David-Neel, *My Journey to Lhasa*, pp. 280–1
9. Taring, *Daughter of Tibet*, p. 81
10. Bass, *Inside the Treasure House*, p. 127
11. Harrer, *Return to Tibet*, pp. 124–6
12. Waddell, *Lhasa and Its Mysteries*, pp. 338–9
13. Ibid., pp. 330-1
14. David-Neel, *My Journey to Lhasa*, pp. 263–4
15. Waddell, *Lhasa and Its Mysteries*, p. 394
16. Ibid., p. 376
17. Ibid., p. 376
18. Ibid., p. 379
19. Harrer, *Seven Years In Tibet*, p. 177
20. Bernard, *Penthouse of the Gods*, pp. 256–8
21. Bernard, private papers
22. Bernard, *Penthouse of the Gods*, p. 337
23. Ibid., pp. 258-9
24. Harrer, *Seven Years In Tibet*, pp. 224–5
25. Harrer, *Return to Tibet*, p. 164
26. Bernard, *Penthouse of the Gods*, p. 264
27. Harrer, *Seven Years in Tibet*, p. 181

28. Waddell, *Lhasa and Its Mysteries*, pp. 372–3

29. David-Neel, *My Journey to Lhasa*, pp. 276–7

30. Waddell, *Lhasa and Its Mysteries*, pp. 343–5

31. Bernard, *Penthouse of the Gods*, p. 250

32. Waddell, *Lhasa and Its Mysteries*, p. 345

33. Bernard, Unpublished diary, Sept. 20, 1937

34. Taring, *Daughter of Tibet*, p. 308

35. Harrer, *Seven Years In Tibet*, pp. 210–11

36. Taring, *Daughter of Tibet*, pp. 179–80

37. Bernard, Unpublished letter, July, 1937

38. Taring, *Daughter of Tibet*, pp. 67–8

39. Ibid., pp. 48–9

40. Ibid., pp. 237–8

41. Waddell, *Lhasa and Its Mysteries*, p. 375

42. Bernard, *Penthouse of the Gods*, p. 240

43. Harrer, *Seven Years In Tibet*, p. 214

44. Bernard, *Penthouse of the Gods*, pp. 185–6

45. Harrer, *Seven Years In Tibet*, p. 247

46. Ibid., pp. 213–4

47. Bernard, Unpublished diary

48. Bernard, *Penthouse of the Gods*, p. 30

49. Ibid., p. 74

50. David-Neel, *My Journey to Lhasa*, pp. 73–4

51. Bernard, *Penthouse of the Gods*, p. 138

52. Waddell, *Lhasa and Its Mysteries*, p. 298

53. Ibid., pp. 300–1

54. Bernard, *Penthouse of the Gods*, p. 137

55. Taring, *Daughter of Tibet*, pp. 194–5

56. Harrer, *Return to Tibet*, p. 142

57. Harrer, *Seven Years in Tibet*, p. 77–79

58. Taring, *Daughter of Tibet*, pp. 26–7

59. Pamphlet in author's collection

60. Waddell, *Lhasa and Its Mysteries*, pp. 199–200

61. French, *Younghusband*, p. 193

62. Ibid., p. 217

63. Bernard, *Penthouse of the Gods*, p. 62

64. Waddell, *Lhasa and Its Mysteries*, pp. 219–20

65. Bernard, *Penthouse of the Gods*, p. 63

66. Waddell, *Lhasa and Its Mysteries*, pp. 230–1

67. Bernard, Unpublished diary, May 27, 1937

68. Waddell, *Lhasa and Its Mysteries*, pp. 232–3

69. Foster, *Forbidden Journey*, pp. 175–6

70. David-Neel, *Magic and Mystery in Tibet*, pp.146–7

71. Ibid., p. 152

72. Bernard, *Penthouse of the Gods*, p. 48

73. David-Neel, *Magic and Mystery in Tibet*, p. 153–4

74. Taring, *Daughter of Tibet*, pp. 51–2

75. David-Neel, *Magic and Mystery in Tibet*, 1965 Introduction

76. Bernard, Unpublished diary, Sept. 28, 1937

77. Harrer, *Return to Tibet*, p. 144

78. Ibid., p. 144

79. Shoumatoff, Vanity Fair

80. Ibid.

81. Bernard, unpublished diary, September 30, 1937

82. David-Neel, *Magic and Mystery in Tibet*, pp. 222–3

GLOSSARY

Avalokiteshwara – (Sanskrit) Buddha of Compassion

Barkor – market area surrounding the Jokhang, Lhasa

Bon – pre-Buddhist, animistic religion of Tibet; (still practiced by many Tibetans and recently recognized as the 5th school of Tibetan Religion)

Chakpori – Hill in Lhasa, former site of medical colleges

Champa – Buddha of the future, *Maitreya* in Sanskrit

Chang – home brewed barley beer

Chenresig – Buddha of compassion, *Avalokiteshwara* in Sanskrit

Chubba – Tibetan robe, often made of sheepskin

Chode – monastary, religious place

Chorten – an eight-tiered shrine, *stupa* in Sanskrit

Drokpa – nomads, often from the northern Tibetan plains

Drepung – monastery near Lhasa, formerly largest in Tibet

Dzo – a hybrid of yak and cow

Dzong – fort, administrative center of many villages, usually built on highest prominence in the area

Ganden – monastery east of Lhasa

Geshe – learned teacher, roughly equivalent of Ph.D. in theology

Gompa – monastery

Gompchen – head (abbot) of a monastery

Gonggar – monastery and small village near Lhasa airport

Gyantse – third largest city in Tibet, south of Lhasa

Jetsuma – title meaning "learned lady"

Jokhang – oldest and holiest Buddhist shrine in Lhasa

Kengyur and Tengyur – books of teaching of the Buddha (*sutras*) and commentaries on them

Kale-kale – slowly-slowly

Kashag – lay political body that governed Lhasa/Tibet

Kathag – ceremonial (offering) scarf

Kham – province in southeastern Tibet

Khampa – person from the province of Kham

Kichyu – river at southern edge of Lhasa

La gyalo – exclamation praising the gods

Latzas – poles for prayer flags

Lhamo – a traditional Tibeten dramatic opera

Losar – Tibetan new year

Lung-gom-pa – persons adept at long distance trance walking

Mani – from "om mani padme hum" indicates the prayer written or chiselled on stones

Mantra – short, formulaic prayer

Mo – divination, formerly practiced by red hat sect lamas

Ngondrol – practices preparatory for further spiritual studies

Norbulinka – summer residence of the Dalai Lama, a palace amid gardens, three miles from Potala

Om mani padme hum – Tibetan prayer (mantra) roughly translated as "a jewel in the lotus"; many extended interpretations of this phrase

Panchen Lama – head of Tashilungpo monastery, Shigatse; second in importance to the Dalai Lama

Philang – foreigner

Potala – palace of the Dalai Lama in Lhasa

Pundits – name given to British trained Indian nationals who worked as spies in Tibet

Ramoche – ancient shrine/monastery in Lhasa

Rinpoche – a monk recognized as a reincarnation

Sera – monastery near Lhasa

Sengyur – a Bon shaman

Shalu – monastery between Gyanste and Shigatse

Shappé – lay political official, member of the Kashag, roughly Cabinet Minister

Shigatse – second largest city in Tibet, West of Lhasa

Sutra – book of the teachings of Buddha

Tashi deleg – Tibetan greeting

Tashilungpo – large monastery in Shigatse

Thanka – sacred scroll painting

Tsakali – eight auspicious symbols of Buddha

Tsampa – flour made from roasted barley

Tsang – Province of Tibet of which Shigatse is capital

Tsangpo – River in southern Tibet, becomes the Brahmaputra in India

Tserpu – monastery about 60 miles from Lhasa

Tumo – the ability to warm oneself through meditative techniques

Yerpa – site of meditation caves and formerly a monastery

Yomdok Tso – large lake between Gyantse and Lhasa.

JUNE CALENDER, A PLAYWRIGHT WHO HAS HAD PRODUC-
TIONS IN NEW YORK CITY AND OTHER U.S. LOCATIONS, WAS
BORN ON A SMALL FARM IN RURAL INDIANA AND RECEIVED HER
BA AT INDIANA UNIVERSITY. AFTER TRAVELING TO TIBET AND
THE HIMALAYAS, MS. CALENDER WROTE PHANTOM
VOICES IN TIBET, HER FIRST NONFICTION BOOK.